MF

**Books should be returned on or before the
last date stamped below.**

14 NOV 2005

24 JUL 2006 HEADQUARTERS

30. APR 07.   0 6 NOV 2012

03. JAN 08.
26. SEP 08.

07 MAY 09

03. FEB 10.

05. OCT 10.

05. AUG 11.

09. SEP 16.

18. MAY 17.

24. JAN 18.

16 JUL 2019

30. JUL 19.

11 APR 13   ABERDEENSHIRE
16. NOV   LIBRARY &
18. NOV   INFORMATION SERVICES

WITHDRAWN
27. AUG 14 FROM LIBRARY

19. MAY
09. FEB 16.

A LITTLE LESS THAN KIND

A LITTLE LESS THAN KIND

Charlotte Armstrong

This Large Print book is published by BBC Audiobooks Ltd, Bath, England and by Thorndike Press®, Waterville, Maine, USA.

Published in 2004 in the U.K. by arrangement with the author's estate.

Published in 2004 in the U.S. by arrangement with Brandt & Hockman Literary Agents, Inc.

U.K. Hardcover ISBN 0–7540–9667–X (Chivers Large Print)
U.S. Softcover   ISBN 0–7862–6526–4 (General)

The text of this Large Print edition is unabridged.
Other aspects of the book may vary from the original edition.

Set in 16 pt. New Times Roman.

Printed in Great Britain on acid-free paper.

British Library Cataloguing in Publication Data available

Library of Congress Control Number: 2004101993

CHAPTER ONE

The receptionist, with her salaried smile, looked up and read the silhouette against the glass. 'Good morning, Mr. Cunningham. We haven't seen you for a long time.' Then she could have bit her tongue.

The boy's slight figure moved towards her on the carpet until she could see him clearly, immaculate in handsome slacks and sports shirt, bearing his bare head bent very slightly to the right, as he always had, his face yellowish (or perhaps not. This light was terrible), the dark hair descending upon his domed forehead in the familiar peninsula. He said in a soft and diffident voice which nevertheless had a pleasing suggestion of unleashed melodic power, 'Hi, Miss Ellis. I'm expected, I think.'

'That's right. You're to go right up to your . . .' This time she did bite her tongue. '. . . stairs,' she said.

The boy turned docilely to the wide stairway that was the chief decoration of this lower lobby, a stairway that began in the middle of the floor without visible support and turned upon a suspended landing, lined with planter-boxes.

Hob Cunningham used to hoot at the artificial greenery. 'Why does a nut and bolt factory have to look like a tropical forest, I ask you?' he used to say, in all good humour. He used to slog it up those stairs and cross the landing, batting at the huge leaves with his blunt hand, amused by their serviceable elasticity. 'One thing, you can't kill 'em,' he used to say.

His son went up and across and up again, sedately.

The woman at the desk on the floor above, a fierce fifty-five, had been here before the building was. 'Hi, there, Ladd,' she greeted him with the privilege of tenure. 'Nice to see you. How are you?'

'I'm just fine, Margaret.' The boy's voice was in control. His whole body was stiff with control. 'Shall I?'

'Sure enough. Go right on in.'

She thought, conventionally, Poor kid. (She shook off a creeping underthought. So, at last he takes the trouble?) When he had gone, she took care to sigh.

*   *   *

There was only one office at this level. Large, luxurious, much-glassed, it rode before and above the series of low saw-toothed roofs, as if it were a lookout tower. Hob Cunningham, ensconced here behind his mammoth desk, had always seemed to be both figuratively and literally on top of the works.

2

There were two men in Hob's officc now, neither of whom was Hob, neither of whom rose for their junior. 'Ah, there you are, Ladd,' said the man behind the desk, pleasantly. 'Sorry to have made this trouble for you.'

'No trouble, sir.' The boy had dark eyes in a sun-tanned face but his eyelids were very white and half down.

The man behind the desk was fifty years old. His thick cap of hair was almost white but he had been a blond; he did not give the effect of being a white-haired man. He had an etched face, crisp of line. He might have been a scholar, with that face, and his aura of quiet intelligence and good humour. The other man to whom he turned was about the same age, with heavy features, his face bold and soft, as if from passion and compassion.

'Aaron,' said David Crown, 'this is my stepson, Ladd Cunningham. Ladd, this is Dr. Silver.'

The doctor's rump left his chair. These two shook hands.

'Aaron is an old college chum,' said David, noticing how the boy's twenty-year-old face, too young for lines, had whole planes of tension. It occurred to him that here was an opportunity he had not foreseen, a gift of chance. 'You've caught us just before lunch,' he said. 'How about joining us?'

'No, sir, I can't.'

And David was up against the wall. He

3

could not coax, he could not even inquire, but must accept the unexplained. So he said, 'Well, I'm sorry: Sit down, then, and I'll get on with the business of the meeting.' David opened a flat drawer, extracted a cheque-book.

'To the bursar?'

'Yes, sir.' The boy sat down in a green leather chair parallel to its twin where Aaron Silver was sitting.

Beyond the glass and the air conditioning, Southern California lay noisy, dusty, tangy, lively in the September heat. There were hills to be seen from here, and the familiar sense of terrain. But the buzz of life, the sound of immediate man and his traffic, was shut away and the big office was quiet enough so that the faint scratch of David's pen was audible. The boy sat almost without breath.

Dr. Silver spoke. 'I knew your father, too. We were all at school, together. Or, I should say, at the same time. David and Hob and I.'

'Is that so, sir?'

'I was very sorry to hear of his death.'

'Yes, sir.'

'You are in college, are you?'

'Yes, sir. I have been.'

'Where, may I ask?'

'Standford, sir.'

The boy's courtesy was so unresponsive as to be discourteous. David waved the cheque to dry. 'Coming up to his senior year,' he contributed.

'What is your field?' Aaron inquired. 'Your major, I should say?'

But Ladd Cunningham was taking the cheque from his stepfather's fingers. 'Thank you, sir. I'm not sure I'll use it.'

'If you don't use it,' said David, smiling, 'I hope that means you want to tackle Cunningham Company.'

'I'm not sure that I will.' The boy had a cryptic and subtle defiant look. It was as if he said, You can't make me tell you what I'm thinking.

'Either way,' said David. He said to Aaron, 'Ladd's mother and I would like to see him get his Bachelor's, at least. A Master's would be even better. But Hob would have understood and been delighted.' A pressure went up in the room as plainly as if a barometer had jumped in their sight. David said to the boy, with challenge, 'If you want to come in here, right now, and learn it the hard way, then start tomorrow.'

'The hard way?' The boy's voice was very soft and breathy.

David smiled. 'That's right,' he said gently. 'If you were to take say some Business Administration, or even, as your mother has suggested, go on to Harvard School of Business, that might shorten the period of practical apprenticeship. But there has to be one.'

'Maybe he would prefer a profession,' said

Aaron mildly.

'If he does he has only to say . . .' The phone rang. David took it. 'Hold my calls, Edna.'

The boy had his feet flat on the floor and close together. He shifted them, ready to rise. 'You're on your way to lunch. I'd better get on my horse.'

'Wait a minute,' David said. 'Just a minute. There's something else.' David got up and went towards the solid wall where at one side of the entrance door it was thickened to contain a fully furnished bathroom, and at the other, a large storage closet. He went into the closet. He was thinking, I want Aaron to get a little longer taste of the quality of this boy.

Aaron said, good-naturedly, 'You haven't answered my question.'

'What question was that, sir?' The boy was in a fever to be off.

'About your major? Your interests?'

The boy's eyes had been flighty. Now they focused. 'I think I remember Dad mentioning your name.'

'We didn't meet often,' said Aaron smoothly. 'We always meant to do better.'

'It's too late, now,' the boy said calmly.

'Is your mother well?' Aaron said. 'I knew her, too—at least slightly, long, long ago.'

'She's fine, thank you,' the boy said. His voice thinned. It became the careful vibration of one string.

David came out of the closet carrying a

6

black cardboard box, a twelve-inch cube. 'I wish you'd take this along, Ladd, since it belongs to you.'

The boy said nothing. He stood up and took the box into both hands.

'And I'm sorry I forgot to leave the cheque this morning as your mother asked me to do. Thanks for coming.'

The boy said, 'I'm supposed to mail it today.'

'And will you?' David was taller than his stepson, and thicker. He smiled down.

The boy smiled sideways up. 'I think I'll *mail* it.'

'Maybe you'd like to poke around the plant, while you're here?'

'Some other time.' The boy began to walk. He looked back over his shoulder and said, 'I'm glad to have met you, Dr. Silver.'

'Thank you.'

'I suppose I'll see you again. So long, then.'

The boy, with the box in his hands, left them. He left on the air the echo of an impudence, very faint, but saucy. It was as if he had said, I see through all this, you know. You don't fool me, either of you.

*   *   *

'He knows what's in the box?' said Aaron.

'You notice he didn't ask?' David settled into the chair behind the desk and blew out his

7

breath. 'He wouldn't ask *me* the time of day. Is that natural?'

Aaron looked tired. 'If you mean is it common, yes. If you mean is it inevitable, no. What is in the box?'

'In the box? Oh, stuff I cleared away from Hob's desk. It could have waited. I wanted you . . .'

'From me, a little friendly witch-doctoring?' said Aaron affectionately.

David leaned back against the comforting resistance of the springs in the chair. His mind was comfortable against the memory of long hours of young argument on great questions with this person. 'I have the executive's virtue. I listen to experts.'

'This is the first time he's been here since his father's death? Or seen you in that chair?'

'That's right.'

'He seemed to have it built up as an ordeal.'

'I understand that, well enough. But why won't he tell us what he intends to do with himself? Because he knows it teases?'

'I see it teases,' Aaron said slyly.

'The fact is, he is going to have to do one of two things. Either go back to school and get involved with his peers and live his life. Or jump in here and apply himself until he can take over where Hob left off.' Launched into this exposition, David already felt relief. He was a man whose mind, with pleasure and from long habit, made thoughtful decisions.

8

To add up pros and cons, to devise a plan and then follow it, was natural to him. At the same time, he knew that not all minds operated in just this way. He had *been* patient. Now, he let off some of his human exasperation. 'What the boy had better not do is hang around the place, moping.'

'What place?'

'The house.'

'Is that what he does there?'

'As far as I can see.'

'It bothers you that he won't choose one of two alternatives you have laid before him?' said Aaron in a creamy voice.

David grinned at him. 'Certainly. Since one of those alternatives includes just about all the choices open to a successful life. If he has a third alternative in mind and thinks I should get out of this chair and let him sit down, today, then that wouldn't bother me. I know I can't turn Hob's business over to a green youth, whether he knows it or not. He couldn't cope.'

'I believe you,' Aaron said dryly. 'Tell me, did you plan this encounter?'

'As a matter of fact, I did not.'

'He thinks that you did.'

'Yes, I noticed. Well, of course, he's . . .'

'Suspicious? Resentful?'

'What really bothers me, Aaron,' said David, 'is that I can't seem to do anything about it. I wonder . . .'

'. . . wonder whether you are guilty?'

David looked fondly at his friend. 'I have a hunch that in your business there is no such thing as yes or no. Shall I tell you about it, Doctor?'

Aaron took his pipe out and began to fill it. 'Well, why not?'

'Where'll I start?' said David, struggling to overcome a momentary reluctance.

'I'm not a Freudian. Skip the womb. Sure you want your calls held?'

David made a cancelling motion of his hand. He thought to himself, This is fair enough. If I want Aaron to advise me, then he'd better know the whole situation, beginning with the way I see it.

'You remember Hob from the old days?' he asked (remembering).

'Loud, quick, smart, fuming with energy. Big man on the campus.'

'He didn't seem to try to be. Rose to the top, like cream on the milk bottle.'

'Old-fashioned unhomogenised milk,' said Aaron. 'Excuse that. Sure, I remember Hob. You and he were brothers, in those days. He ran around with Abigail Ladd. He was gown and she was town.'

'That's right. But it so happens, that during the years I was in law school and Hob gone, I ran around with Abigail Ladd. So it is that old.'

'Turn you down, did she, Dave?'

10

'It so happened I didn't ask her. I went to war. Hob, of course, had gone off to see the world, and turned up in Spain at the right time—or the wrong time—whichever way you want to look at it. He smelled the hot war sooner than most of us. Oh, he was in. When he got out, in 1944, he went right back, found Abby, and married her.'

'Hob beat you home, then?'

'Well, no, that's not quite the way it was, either,' said David, smiling. 'See, June and I had the words said one rainy Saturday afternoon in '42. Couple of crazy Yanks in war-time England, not positively guaranteed to survive. I'd known her a week. And it was marvellous, all the way. Exception that proves the rule, eh?'

'I believe you,' said Aaron gently.

He had better, thought David, seeing pictures. June at Hob's wedding, about as pregnant as she could be and still walking around.

'I was Hob's best man,' he said. 'The way it was, when I got out—I came home to a wife, a daughter-and-a-half, a steady job in my father-in-law's business and the good life.' He glanced up.

'Come on,' said Aaron, reading him. 'I humanly believe that the good life is possible.'

'So long as ye both shall live,' said David starkly.

Aaron dropped the light note immediately.

11

'How old were your girls when their mother died?'

'Sixteen, seventeen. Just heading for college. So I held the fort, kept the house as long as they needed a house. Angie's married to a chap named Sullivan Jones. She's in New York. I've got a grandson, poor little slob—named Davey Jones.'

David was asking for the light note back. Aaron smiled.

'And Patty married one Martin Serafino, architect. Chicago. They're avant-garde, poor but proud—and having a marvellous time. Well . . . it was a big house. Then, the old man being long gone, I'd trained up a couple of young fellows. So I turned in my chips. Came out here. I don't remember, now, what it was I thought I was going to do. I looked up Hob.'

'Winter of last year. I remember.'

'You were in Europe.'

'I remember.'

'I got involved, Aaron. You and Hob . . .'

'Never did. For one thing, Hob's range didn't include psychological theory. He thought the unconscious was something found only in the unfortunate.' Aaron grinned.

David said suddenly, 'I don't like that boy, you know. In full consciousness.'

'Hob's boy?'

'At least, I don't like the wall he puts up, because it defeats me and I will admit to you that I'm not used to that.'

Aaron said nothing. His face was fond.

'You have a son?' David asked him.

'Age fifteen. And a girl twelve. Late start. Six years of war—in the Pacific for the most part. Medical . . .'

David said, 'I never had a son.'

'Resume, please,' said Aaron with a faint sigh. 'You got involved. Where was the boy?'

'Yes. Well . . . I used to go to dinner. Abby, of course . . . The boy was up in Palo Alto. I saw almost nothing of him. As far as I know, he accepted an old friend of the family. In the spring, they found out Hob had cancer. I rallied around better than anybody else they knew—being free. There was surgery. Ladd came home and was told that the operation was a success. Which was no lie, at the time. So he went off with some pals on a jaunt to Mexico City. Hob staggered through the summer. Ladd was home in August, back to school in late September. Hob went back in the hospital in October. By that time, I was thoroughly involved.'

And that was a long enough list of dates and places, thought David. It was not 'telling.' 'To the best of my knowledge,' said David, carefully, 'I loved them both. I am in love with Abby. Did I tell you? In spite of my age, her age—although it's not the same . . .'

'How could it be?' said Aaron.

'Yes. Well, Abby is a very feminine female.' (Abby has nerves and needs. And Abby, in

13

need, is pretty irresistible. She creates a vacuum and all your noblest instincts rush in to fill it.) David smiled, half at himself.

'She needs a rock. Hob knew it, because he was her rock. I'd better tell you, now, what Hob said to me. If we are on the question of my guilt.'

Aaron said nothing.

'Here's Hob, this dynamo,' burst David, 'and the thing squeezing his life out from the inside.' He veered. 'Now, in the spring, I forgot to say, this business was in crisis. And I'll explain to you, Doctor, that a living business is usually in crisis. Seems to be a sign of life. So Hob, in the hospital then, asked me if I'd step in here and be his deputy. He could run it from his bed if he had me on the spot. Hob's got some wild young men in here; they had to be watched. So I became the deputy. Enjoyed it. Still do enjoy it. I stayed all last summer. Hob got down here only once in a while. The story was that he must come back into harness gradually. But gradually, he slipped the other way.' David paused.

'And Hob said to you . . .' Aaron was partner, shadow, following close enough to lead.

'Yes. Hobart Arthur Cunningham, the Second, that brash and wonderful guy, was dying. And knew it. Abby hadn't come, that night. He said to me, "Dave, somebody's got to keep Cunningham Company intact for Abby.

14

And for the boy. Will you do it?"

' "I'll do what I can," I told him.

' "Then you'll do it," Hob said. "I don't know," he said, "whether the boy will ever want it—to run, that is. If he turns to it, fine. If he's got another way to go, then let him go his way. But I don't want Abby worried, cheated, or ever low in the financial department. She never has been in her life, Dave, and I haven't worked all my life, to let that happen. So you take Cunningham Company. Bring it along. Do this for me? On salary, of course," Hob said. "Give yourself a raise."

'I said I would. I said I thought I was worth it.

'He said, "Teach the boy, when and if he wants to learn."

' "That I will," I told him.

' "Or if not, then when there is a propitious time, sell it out and fix Abby to be safe. Do this for me?"

'I said I would. You know, that wasn't easy. He was—emaciated. If you've ever seen it . . .'

'I've seen it,' said Aaron.

'Yes. Well, then Hob looked at the wall and this is what he said. "It's real nice," he said, "to make a will when you're checking out, and nice to figure that your will is going to be done. Although I don't think it can be . . . not altogether. Still, I'm going to tell you, Dave, what would be my will if I could have it. I'd leave Abby to you."

15

'I told him I'd look after Abby.

' "I know," Hob said. "But what I meant . . . I want you to support her. She's that kind of woman. She needs support. Dave, she's suggestible. She's sensitive. I don't want to leave her, but since I'm leaving, I don't want her *left*. If I could have my will . . ." Oh, he turned around and gave it to me, straight. "I'd have her clinging where I *know*. Would you be willing to marry Abby?"

'I stammered something. Hob raised up. He said, "Excuse me. I know I can't arrange a thing like that. I only want the two of you to be sure. If such a thing should happen, it's fine with me." He looked like death.

'So I said to Hob, "Listen, for God's sake, don't talk like that to Abby!"

' "Why not?" he asked me. You remember the shrewd look his eyes used to have? and his long nose in the air?

'I said, "You could spoil my chances, you old fool!"

'And Hob lay back. I thought he'd been—eased.' David gazed blindly out at the hills. 'That was two days after Thanksgiving. Four days after Thanksgiving, he—just died.'

'He did not talk to Abby about it?'

'No. I told her the gist, later on. After we had married.'

'Why didn't you want Hob to tell her?'

'Because I didn't want Abby to think that Hob had put the notion into my head.'

16

'Why not?'

'Because he hadn't,' David said flatly.

Aaron took the pipe from his mouth and nodded comfortably. 'When did you fall in love with her?'

'How would I know, Doctor? It got up into my conscious mind, oh, late that summer.'

'So you had thought of marriage?'

'Yes. I was lonely. She had need. I foresaw.'

'Had you been wishing Hob would die?'

'Of course,' said David.

'All right,' said Aaron in a moment. 'I've seen what they call "terminal" cases.'

'It could have been worse,' said David sadly, 'or so I am told. Hob is supposed to have escaped some of the modern keep-the-corpse-theoretically-alive routines. But it was bad enough.'

'Go on. Especially about the boy.'

'When Hob died the boy was shocked, subdued, and just as glad, I thought, that somebody else was taking the brunt. He stayed at school. I threw my weight around this plant. Stood by Abby. Well, I courted her. It was a long and fascinating winter, last winter. In May, Abby and I were married. The boy didn't come down for the wedding, which was no great social occasion, just the knot tied in the minister's study.'

'In May?'

'Seems soon?' said David cheerfully. 'Ah, but not to have married might have caused

17

worse talk. We were . . . very close by then.'

'All right.'

'Ladd had known all along . . . or he should have known, what was going on. Maybe he just didn't pay attention. Anyway, the moment the date was set, we both wrote. He sent congratulations and best wishes. But he said he had finals. I don't know. We thought he was living his life. We were not offended.' David's mouth twitched.

'Had Hob spoken about a possible marriage to his son, do you know?'

'I doubt it. I'm pretty sure not. No time. He wouldn't have done that before he spoke to me. And Hob . . . Well, he was a father who assumed that the boy would leave the nest and live his life. As Hob had done.'

'But the boy is in the nest, eh?'

'He's been home since early August. Went to the mountains with some college types, early part of this summer. That's been his pattern. Now, by the pattern, he ought to be going back next week. But he won't say that he will. Or that he won't. I've tried to discuss it, tried to wait and be patient, tried to establish some kind of liveable ease between us, but the truth is, I am just not getting anywhere. Any suggestions?'

'For yourself?'

'Naturally, for me.'

'The intruder?'

'I may *be,*' said David, vehemently, 'but here

18

I am. So, don't toy with any suggestion that I step out, drop the works on the kid. Let him wreck the business. Let him try to support Abby which—in Hob's sense—he cannot do. Leave Abby to the mercies of I don't know what.'

'It would be a nice revenge,' said Aaron thoughtfully.

David looked at him and felt his scalp move and his face change. 'I didn't say I hated the boy. Love him, no.'

'In my business, love and hate are not black and white.'

'Everybody is a dirty grey, eh?' said David teasingly. 'All right, then that's what I am.' He watched his friend expectantly a moment, but his friend said nothing. 'Lunch?' David picked up his phone. 'What's pending, Edna? Anything crucial?' He dealt with what was pending.

When he hung up, he rose but his guest did not. Aaron said musingly, 'You know, Dave, there was a time when a young fellow who wanted to get married went to the girl's papa and asked permission to try for her hand.'

'Yes?'

'Quaint, eh? But it may be that, in those days, a lot of little dragons were slain before they could grow up to be big dragons.'

David sat down abruptly. 'You speak of the days when the parents could say No and make it stick?'

Aaron stretched his eyes. 'Not—necessarily.'

'Then I don't buy it,' said David. 'A sop? No, I did not ask the boy's permission, because he did not have the power to say No.'

'An honest man,' said Aaron, beginning to squint his eyes and tilt his head.

'What are you doing?'

'Trying to judge the impression you make. You look pretty good, Dave. A little too good, maybe. Where did you get that face?'

'I look like my father,' said David, in surprise. 'What are you driving at?'

'You could be the cream of western civilisation. Or a super-hypocrite. If they are not the same thing.' David stared at him.

'Where Hob was loud, you are quiet. You are just as smart, but smoother. You seem to lead a more examined life. In fact, you display all the most respected virtues of our age. Reasonable. Kind. Honest. Patient. And understanding. I'm trying to see through the boy's eyes.'

'Then you're not doing it very well,' snapped David. 'To him, I look like an old creep.'

'Yes,' said Aaron softly.

David got up. 'I thought you said you weren't a Freudian. Let's eat.' On the way to the door, he said, 'Can anybody help the boy through this? Could you?'

'Not while he is happy.'

'Happy?'

'Nothing like a strong hatred to integrate the personality—temporarily. No, Dave, seriously . . . When and if he knows he needs some help, then someone might. Probably not I. Or it may suddenly leave him, roll up like a cloud and lift away.

'How?'

'God knows,' said Aaron. 'It works *in* him, you see? We can't know how. Or whether he is, at all, aware.'

'Steady does it, eh?'

'What else?' said Aaron.

All right, thought David. Up again, old heart.

CHAPTER TWO

Ladd Cunningham drove his Corvette home, too fast for town streets. Displaying his virtuosity, he whipped into the long driveway without slackening speed, and zoomed between the high grey stucco house on his right and the pool enclosure on his left, screaming to a stop precisely upon the mark, under the carport. He got out and took up the black box from the floor of his car. The young people on the pool deck were shouting 'Hi'— he didn't want to answer. He had to keep his back turned towards the open triple garage where stood his mother's car, the empty space

21

for his stepfather's car and that other car, never used now, that stood nearest the garden wall, covered with parachute cloth as if it wore a shroud.

His mother had asked him once if he would like to drive it. But he didn't want to drive it. He didn't want to see it. The sight of it tied him in knots. Why didn't they sell it? Didn't do his father's Caddy any good to sit there. Rotting.

With the box under his arm, he sidled towards the fence. The Lorimers were in there and Gary Fenwick. He didn't want to talk to the Lorimers. He said, 'Hey, Gare?'

'Hey, Ladd?'

'Come on up.'

'Sure thing.' Gary was huge. He lumbered along the deck, towelling his head.

'Put your pants on,' Ladd said in icy command and turned and walked.

The big L-shaped house, now on his left, stood on ground four feet higher than the driveway and the pool area. Broad steps led up into the garden that lay within the sheltering arms of the L. But Ladd veered away from those steps when he saw his mother and Rafe Lorimer on the quarter circle of brick terrace. They waved and called 'Hi.' He waved but he went on to the kitchen door. Didn't want to talk to them.

'You all had your lunch, Mr. Ladd?' Cleona asked him.

'I don't need any. Where's the beer?' Ladd swung open the refrigerator door and found the cans of beer. He found frankfurters and put one, cold as it was, into his mouth as if it were a cigarette. He had the black box under his arm.

Cleona materialised beside him with a small round tray, so he put four cans of beer on the tray and a couple more frankfurters and a piece of cheese. He balanced the tray on his right hand. Cleona projected some dark inarticulate communication that he sensed and rejected. 'Don't touch me,' his spirit screamed.

He went into the spacious hall, and on the stairs that made a tilted question mark, flowing in beauty, he fled upward.

*   *   *

Felicia Lorimer sat on the pool coping and lifted her brown legs, let them down, watched the blue and crystal movement of water and light swirling in beauty around her ankles.

Her brother, supine on the diving board, said, 'His not to reason why.'

Gary Fenwick had trotted in his beefy way down to the pool house. This was built against a wall protecting the pool from the street, at the other end of the long rectangle. Since childhood, Gary had gone where Ladd Cunningham suggested that they go, played the pranks that Ladd dreamed up, been the muscle for Ladd's brain. Even now that they had been separated during three college years, since Gary lived at home and went to a local college, for financial reasons—even now Gary reacted to the old habit. It did not seem to occur to him to argue, for instance, that this was the perfect sunny day for pool-lounging.

The Lorimers said no more until Gary had reappeared, in shorts and shirt, let himself out of the self-latching gate, and lumbered off towards the house. Felicia leaned back on straight arms and lifted her face to the sunlight, very conscious of her taut little body, her flat tummy, her neat buttocks, her small breasts that were, nevertheless, unmistakably breasts. Her dark hair was wet and hung dismally.

'Hey, Felicia?' Justin said softly.

She didn't want to talk to her brother. His world was a different world from hers. Justin was very well made, smooth skin over long muscles. He was blondly good-looking and he had a flair. He had a ruthless fitness about him and cared nothing for God or the devil.

'What?' she said flatly. But she already knew what. Felicia wasn't a 'cute' girl. Her lips were too full, her nose was too flat, her eyes were too small, and no amount of suntan would change these features. She would never be pretty. She hoped to be attractive. But hers would never be an appeal that a thoroughly well-adjusted bourgeois like her brother Justin

24

could recognise. She was just the tolerated little sister.

'Look,' said her brother to the sky, 'I'm taking off Saturday night.'

'I know it.'

'But Ladd's not going.'

She didn't say anything because her heart jumped.

'Something's taken his mind off education,' said Justin impatiently. 'What I want to say to you is—watch it, and don't mess around with him.'

'I don't know why you say that to me,' said Felicia plaintively. 'Ladd's never even asked me out.'

'Aah . . .' Justin rolled his head upon the fibre mat. She looked up and caught his glance out of his very dark blue eyes. 'Come on,' said Justin Lorimer. 'He isn't dating. He hangs around. So do you. You think I'm stupid or something? He talks. You're dumb enough to listen.'

'It's never dumb to listen.'

'So'—her brother talked her down—' if you're getting ideas about little old Cousin Ladd, I'm telling you to forget them. Because this kid is—'

'What?' said Felicia belligerently.

'Off the beam,' her brother said sharply. 'You stick with your own crowd. Let him alone. Even a pretty-near senior in high school, like you, is not the oldest and wisest character in the world.'

'Off the beam, eh?' said Felicia musingly. 'Because he may have problems and feelings that you don't understand?'

'Don't tell me,' groaned her brother, 'that you're falling for that old sensitive-suffering-soul routine. After what we've been through?'

Felicia held hard to her own mysteries. She slapped her legs upon the water. 'Why the sudden concern?' she said flippantly. 'Is it for *my* soul? Or what?'

'Okay. Okay,' her brother said. But he rolled over and she couldn't avoid his dark, his blue, his cool, his too bright gaze. 'I'm not going to be around,' he said, 'and Rafe's been an idiot, all his life. Look, I never was Ladd Cunningham's slave and admirer but I have nothing special against him . . .'

'All other people besides you may not be idiots,' his sister said. She let her shoulders hunch up to support her skull. Her full lips were drawn into a smile.

Her brother said, 'In one ear and out the other. Okay. It figures.' He put his face down on his folded arms and surrendered to the beating sunshine.

Felicia felt that her brother didn't believe in suffering, nor did he listen to tiny clues, prophetic whispers. Whole dimensions of life were sealed from him.

'*Que sera sera,*' she said, feeling very happy, not noticing how she took his intuition for the truth. She believed what she had hoped. Ladd Cunningham would not go away this year. He would stay in the big house that stood back to back with the shabby old frame house where Felicia and her father lived, and her brother, in the summer.

* * *

Up on the terrace, Abigail said to Felicia's father, 'Take pity on the last muffin, please, Rafe?'

Rafe crinkled up his whole face, top to bottom, in the way he had. 'Cleona is a menace to mankind. Can't you stop her from baking muffins?'

'I really don't try,' said Abby, who was still miraculously slim and fair.

Rafe took the last muffin and spread it lavishly with all the rest of the butter. His grey hair stood up on his head. He was wearing a grey sweat shirt and a pair of cotton slacks, washed colourless. Sandals on his bare feet. He was sixty odd, and in some vague way a cousin of Abigail's. He was in and out of her house, and his children in and out of her pool, as naturally as cat and kittens. Rafe lived frugally on some income from his dead wife's estate and never asked Abby for anything, but Abby was carelessly generous.

Rafe had a philosophy. Never worry about money. So when Hob Cunningham had

27

slipped Rafe a cheque one day, in an amount to cover four years' tuition at Stanford for Justin, Rafe had accepted it with gracious secrecy, put it in Justin's bank account, with a covering lie, and since had forgotten all about it. He was, complacently, a secessionist. No rat race for Rafe. He had the old house and the sufficient income and the old stable made into a studio where he sculpted or painted or carved, according to where he felt his talents ought to go, in any given week. He was not greatly talented at any of the arts, but it never occured to Rafe not to be an artist.

Nor did it occur to him that he might not be qualified for the role of wise old counsellor, which he blithely and frequently assumed. He said to Abby, 'I don't think there's anything to worry about. Ladd is just a little confused. He needs time to think. He'll come into his own. Don't fear.'

Abby was a lovely creature. Her brow had a little built-in pucker on it and her big eyes searched faces for reassurance. People tended to reassure Abby. 'I don't know, Rafe,' she said. 'He seems so especially moody and so far away. Of course, Ladd never has been a completely sunny personality.'

'Brilliant boy. Brilliant boy,' murmured Rafe.

'Do you think he is mourning for Hob, still?'

'Why, Hob's passing has had an effect, naturally. Perhaps being at home. But all this will pass. It will pass.' Rafe patted her forearm.

Abby sighed. 'I don't know *why* people think that's a comforting remark. It does not comfort *me*. I wish he were happier right now, Rafe. I don't like feeling that even I can't reach my son any more.'

'Growing pains. Growing pains, dear Abby. Children grow away. You wouldn't believe the contempt in which my son holds me at the moment. It's a phase.'

'It doesn't bother you?'

'No, no, no.' Rafe slurped coffee. 'They all go through that. Of course, my Felicia . . .' He cocked his head. Abby had shifted her narrow feet. She never had taken to Felicia for some reason, as everyone knew. 'Do you know,' said Rafe, blinking rapidly, 'I have had an idea. Now, it isn't spring,' he continued in his somewhat coy manner, 'but just the same a young man's fancy . . .'

'You don't think what's bothering Ladd is a girl!'

'Well . . . now . . . it could be.'

'But what girl?'

'Well . . . now . . . who can say?'

'Oh dear, if that were all,' said Abby.

Rafe said, 'Not to worry.' His breast was swelling with wise and well-intended plots. 'We'll see. We'll see.'

'Of course,' said Abby, 'I suppose that's possible. I hadn't thought. We are all so vain, aren't we? We always think it must be something we have done.'

'My dear, my dear,' said Rafe beaming, 'you've done no wrong.'

'I've never meant to.'

'Nor ever have,' Rafe comforted. Tears fell out of Abby's eyes. He touched her hand. 'It's not easy to be young, remember?'

'It's not easy to be middle-aged, either,' said Abby, and then her fine eyes, full of tears, began to laugh at herself, which was one of Abby's charms.

*   *   *

Ladd's room in the rearward arm of the L was now the half that faced away from the garden and the pool. He had changed rooms, this summer. He used to be in the other half, with the southern sun upon his windows, facing inward upon the establishment, getting an angular line of sight upon the other arm of the L, and the windows of his parents' bedroom. Now, he could look over the neighbour's roof, north to the hills. Although he didn't often look out of the window.

His mother had let him fix this room as he pleased: he'd got rid of a lot of kid stuff. Every piece of furniture was very low—the divan-bed close to the floor, the couch low-slung. Ladd was lying on the carpet, itself. Gary, sprawled, face down, on the couch, was beating time as the hi-fi blasted.

When the player stopped, Gary said idly, 'Hey, Ladd, what's in that box?'

'I don't know.'

'Why don't you look?'

'Because I don't care. Listen, Gare. You know what he had laid on for a trap?'

'What?'

'A psychiatrist.'

'Huh!'

'Oh, you bet.'

'Listen . . .'

'Don't believe it, then. A Jew-boy, he had there. Doctor Silver.' Ladd's thin mouth had a bitter line. 'Maybe you better cut out,' Gary said mildly.

'No, I can't.'

'Cunningham Company, eh?'

'I can't.'

'Going to State with me? Hey, neat!'

Ladd rolled his head. 'The hard way, he says. The hard way. He made it the hard way, oh, did he not? He got married!'

Gary said, 'How about some Dixieland?' He heaved himself over to the hi-fi.

'I want long-hair.'

Gary said, with a blank look, 'Sure.'

Ladd rolled on the carpet, in restless misery. There was nothing on earth—nothing—that he wanted. Except vague everything. His fingers touched the black box and he flipped the lid off.

As Gary started the music and retreated to

listen, Ladd sat up slowly. He pulled the box within his reach and under his eyes. On top, there was a photograph, framed in gold. It was Abigail, young and beautiful. *With all my love* was written across her bosom in Abby's spiky hand. Her son took the photograph out of the box and put it on the carpet, face down. *All,* he thought bitterly, a drumming in his ears that wasn't the music.

Another photograph. Ladd himself. His high school senior picture. Young, callow, oblivious, fatuously happy and callow. He turned his own face to the floor with a pang of disgust. A pen. Fancy desk pen, with its anchoring gadget. Black and gold. A paper weight, heavy square of onyx. Then a . . . what?

A stone. A grey stone, pinkveined. Of a certain shape. A shape that fit and comforted the hand.

The boy sat cross-legged on the floor and the stone fit into his hand and he remembered.

One time . . . one time . . . father and son at the beach. Hob had never been the pal-type Dad, but one time he and Ladd had made an expedition. Ladd had been eleven or twelve—something like that. They had gone to the beach, a beach of stones, a place where rumour had it that sometimes, after certain tides, moonstones were to be found, having washed to shore.

Why had they gone? Oh yes, Abigail had been down with the 'flu and had Cleona to

32

take care of her. On that Saturday . . .

Hob Cunningham took very little interest in nature, but they had gone, that one time, to this beach in wind and sun. Kidded about finding moonstones to a profit, although neither of them had any idea what a moonstone would look like.

Hob, his big calf muscles tight against the cloth when the breeze hit the trousers of his business suit, laughing. Not indulging anybody. Just Hob Cunningham, amused at himself for being where he was.

Ladd could remember his own sense of strain. Wanting to play his proper part, boy-on-expedition-with-father. But not able. Because Hob was just Hob Cunningham and Ladd just happened to be his son and you couldn't—

Ladd bashed his memories back to the point. The stone. Oh yes, he had collected a whole heap of stones and pebbles to take home. He had brought them home, and thrown them out after a year or two. Hob had taken one stone. This one.

So there had been something significant? After all? After all? Between his hero-father and himself? Or why keep . . .? The stone felt alive. Ladd opened his hand and let it fall. But no one must ever touch it! No one else!

He poked deeper into the box. Inside, he was screaming and dying of a terrible something. A leather-bound book lay at the bottom of the box.

33

Ladd pried it out and opened it. Music streamed into his ears. The book was a kind of daily appointment pad. Something Hob had kept in his desk. It had squiggles and symbols, initials, cryptic self-directed reminders. Ladd turned the pages at random, frightened before the mysterious marks that he could never decipher. Never. Never. Then he found plain writing. His fingers pinched paper. He shut the book with a snap and pinched it in both hands and held it to his forehead.

Startled, Gary said, 'What's the matter?'

The leather was cool on the skin of his forehead; the music was rising to triumph in brass. The moment had content too heavy to bear. Had to move, break it. Ladd leaped up. He stood taller than he really was.

Gary heaved and put his feet to the floor. 'What's wrong?'

'Oh, the fool!' said Ladd with bright eyes.

'Who?'

'David! David! Dear old David! The fool! The fool! Gave this to me!'

'What is it? What's up?'

'But I knew it. That's what I knew. All the time.' Ladd began to move around the room, almost prancing. 'I knew but I didn't know and I don't know how I knew. But I've got it. He gave it to me. Simple as a, b, c, and d . . .' Ladd let out a strange crowing sound. 'So now I know.'

Gary sat on the edge of the couch with his

jaws moving as if he were chewing gum. It was a mannerism he employed when he was bewildered, which was often.

Ladd stood still, becoming tall and taut. 'You're my buddy, buddy?' He was not really thinking of the other boy as a 'buddy' or even as an entity. 'You won't talk.' Ladd made this a statement holding a faint flavour of threat. It was mechanical.

Gary's jaws moved. His head moved in a negative sign.

Ladd burst: he could contain these words no longer. He would have said them to the wall. 'He killed my father. His name is Death.' Ladd sank down into his cross-legged position and bent over as if he had a cramp in his middle. He rocked.

'How do you figure?' said Gary, looking more stupid than astonished.

'Because it's right in here. Because he gave it to me. My father's writing. I've got the message. Oh yes, I read it, loud and clear.'

'What do you mean, killed him? Who did?'

'I mean killed him.' Ladd's monotone went on, 'I mean caused him to become dead. I mean David Crown did it.'

But . . . Hey, Ladd, that's kinda . . . you know . . . serious. Where does it say . . . ?'

'Not going to get away . . . oh, no . . . he's not going to get away . . . thinks he has . . . he hasn't . . . he won't . . .' It was a chant. It was childish.

35

'What are you going to do?'

'Kill him,' said Ladd. He looked up with brilliant eyes.

Now, something of the existence of this other came through to him. He felt no sense of caution but simply of power. Gary would behave exactly as Ladd wanted. 'I'm not going to shoot him,' he said impatiently. 'Shooting's too good for him. I mean, I'll get *rid* of him. And I will. I will.'

Gary said, 'Let me see what it says.'

'No. You don't want to see it, Gare.' Ladd was yellow. The ruddiness had vanished from under his tan. (No one must ever touch this book! No one else!) 'And you're not going to say one word about it. You swear that?'

'What can I say, if you won't . . . ?'

'Swear?'

'Okay, I swear.'

'But whatever I do,' said Ladd strangely, 'you'll know the reason. Don't forget that.'

Gary rubbed his crew cut. 'How could he kill your Dad?' he said in an awestruck fashion.

'So he'd get what he wanted. Which was everything. And he did get everything. And he got it the hard way. Oh, you bet!' Ladd held the book to his breast and toppled. He curled around it on the floor. 'Oh, I'll kill him,' he said almost lightly. He had long lashes. The lashes lifted from his cheeks. Gary stared at his friend. Ladd lay on the floor and stared at

36

nothing. The music stopped.

Gary said, 'How come your father would know about it? I mean, write it down in there?'

'You couldn't read it,' Ladd said. 'I am the only one. Nobody else could read it.' He let go the book with one hand and groped for the stone. It fit into his palm. He closed his eyes. 'My father wanted me to know and now I know, that's all.' A look of satisfaction and relief came down upon his face.

CHAPTER THREE

On Saturday, at a quarter to six, Felicia, who was all ready except for her dress and her shoes, who had been working for an hour with her coiffure, slipped on slippers and a muu-muu, went downstairs and out through the deserted kitchen across the grass to the studio.

Rafe, in his old clothes, was hacking away at an odd-looking piece of wood, a reddish and fibrous log. 'Dad, it's time to dress for dinner.'

'Ah, is it?' He looked at her and after a while his eyes focused. 'This is Saturday? Dress, eh?'

'It isn't just the Cunninghams and us,' Felicia said patiently. 'They've got another guest coming, a Doctor somebody. And anyway, if it's Justin's farewell dinner, you know cousin Abigail is going to make it fancy.'

37

'Yes, I'd better dress.' Rafe hacked with the little hatchet-like device he had in his hand.

'What's that?' It was not enough to have warned him. Felicia knew he was capable of being drawn on into shaping the thing until he forgot the warning and the time. She must get him physically started into the house.

'This?' said Rafe, pleased to have been asked. 'Ah, this is a Tiki-god.'

'A . . . god?' Felicia shivered a little.

'Ah yes. People put them in among the plantings for a garden ornament. But you know, they are so crude . . . easiest thing in the world . . . Do you see?'

Felicia said nothing. She did not move. Rafe looked up, called by her immobility. 'I'm coming,' he said.

Then he smiled, which pushed his face top to bottom like an accordion. Rafe constantly wore an expression of amiable but unsmiling absorption. When he put on the smile, Felicia thought, it was as if he plugged himself in to the currents of society. He lit up. Yet it was put on. It took his will.

She leaned on the door jamb pensively. A golden light lay on the green behind her. But her father was not a lonely man. Or, if he was, he did not know it. He lived in a kind of ivory . . . well . . . at least an ivy tower, she thought fondly, in a world he had invented for himself. And did not know that, either. Rafe was fond of groups, fond of distributing his store of

38

philosophies, not because he was vain but because he was benign. He received a good deal of local respect for his unconventional way of life. For being an artist? No, probably because people could tell that he didn't really need them, after all.

Felicia felt herself to be a truly lonely person—that is, one who needed more attention than she got. Justin was different. If he walked alone it was on other people's attention that he placed his sure and spurning feet.

'Justin,' said Rafe, as if he caught his son's name out of her mind and suddenly remembered that he had a son and the son was going away. 'Packed, I suppose?'

'I guess so.'

'That long drive, alone at night,' Rafe sighed.

'He'd rather,' she said carelessly. None of this was important. They both knew that Justin would do what he would do and do it well. Rafe was not really concerned. He was just in the process of pulling himself away from his puttering.

Or so she thought, until Rafe said, 'Ladd's not going. Why is that? Do you know, dear?'

Felicia did not move, but all her senses were alerted. 'I don't know,' she said in the same careless tone exactly. 'I guess he'd rather not.'

Rafe was putting tools away. But she knew him very well, indeed, and she was alarmed.

'You've spent so much time together, this last while,' her father said, 'I thought perhaps you would have been told.'

She shrugged and slouched against the wood. Oh, no, she thought, no, please, no! Don't let Rafe begin to matchmake or unmatchmake or meddle, at all! Oh no . . . so delicate were the tendrils, so unsubstantial, so easily wiped away by one swipe of a heavy hand. If indeed there existed any tendrils of connection, except those she held suspended in her own creative hope.

'What do you and Ladd talk about?' her father was asking. So kind. So cruel.

'Books, music—nothing,' she murmured. She gazed across his cluttered workroom and out the big window at the far end, through which she caught glimpses of blue water in the Cunninghams' swimming pool. She kept her expression dreamy. She pretended not to be interested in this exchange. What am I going to do? she was thinking, frantically.

'Abby's a little worried. As for me, I never worry, of course. But I do wonder . . .'

'Hm?' said Felicia as if she hadn't been listening.

'I thought perhaps you would know—better than anyone,' Rafe said slyly. 'Look at me, pet.'

Felicia blinked. She saw the log with the crude face half hacked out upon it. Her lids went down. 'Dad,' she said on a low plaintive

40

note, 'could I ask you something?'

'Anything, darling.'

'I don't want to upset you,' Felicia said. She looked up—wide-eyed, troubled. Oh, she had his attention and it was mean to manipulate . . . to turn his attention . . . but it was so easy and she knew how to do it. She had to do it to save herself.

'I just wonder if it's right,' she said, 'to imitate some people's religious symbol for an ornament.' She straightened and launched into exposition. 'I mean, what if a symbol of yours . . . I won't say the cross because you don't go to church . . . but what if on some island, some place, people were using the American flags—well—for tea towels? They'd be very pretty.'

Her father's face was brick-red. He pulled his chin in. His hair seemed to stand up even more than usual. Perhaps it was the redness of his scalp. 'No, darling, it is not right,' Rafe said with great dignity.

She had known where to strike. She loved him very much and she had known just what to do, but now she flew to him and into his arms. Rafe, for all his informal garb, was a clean and a sweet-smelling man. 'Daddy, I'm sorry. I know other people do it. Maybe I'm silly. I had to *say*.' She was tearful for her own duplicity.

Rafe stroked her hair, ruining the hard-wrought coiffure. Felicia let it go without protest . . . 'You must always say what you

41

think to me,' he comforted. 'My happiness,' he added tenderly, playing on her name.

In his daughter's ear was the slow sound of his heart. Oh God, she thought, why do things have to be the way they are? What is the matter with people?

Ladd Cunningham stood in the open door and said, 'Excuse me. Did Gary come by your driveway?'

The sun was a little lower. He was a grey shape against the light. He had barked the question.

Rafe let Felicia go. 'Why . . . I haven't seen him. Have you, dear?'

'No,' said Felicia.

Ladd began to withdraw.

'About to dress and appear,' called Rafe genially. 'We'll see you at dinner.'

'Yes, I'm looking forward,' said Ladd on a strange ringing note. Then he vanished.

'What does he want with Gary?' said Rafe, blinking.

'Oh, Gary's coming to dinner, too,' said Felicia. 'Cleona told me. Abby was practically weeping over her table. So she asked Gary to make eight. As if it matters.'

Rafe patted her shoulder. 'Poor Abby.' He knew Felicia wasn't crazy about Cousin Abby.

They walked together towards the house. Poor Abby, thought Felicia with scorn. She knew very well that three years ago, when her own mother, Sylvia, had died, Abby had wanted to take a little girl under her wing. Teach her to dress, to have manners, bring her up the way Abby thought she should go. But Felicia had quietly wiggled out of that relationship. Eluded it. Abby was a lady. Felicia admitted and even admired that. But Felicia had been an ugly duckling and an ugly duckling has its own destiny. Felicia didn't want to be a lady. She didn't . . . at least not any more . . . even want to be a 'cute' girl. Felicia was going to have to be Felicia, whatever that was. She tried to be sorry that Abby was miffed, but Abby must let her alone.

Now Felicia began to turn, on her sympathies, the tone of Ladd's voice. How would I feel, she thought, if Rafe had married . . . say, Cousin Abby? I would feel as if everything was falling to pieces and I would know there was nothing I could do about it and I would just hate it. It would take me a long time to get used to it at all.

David said, 'We'll sneak a cocktail.'

*　　　*　　　*

The big drawing-room, that took all of the rearward L of the house, held only the two of them. Abby had welcomed Dr. Silver in her charming way and then excused herself to fuss over her table. No other guests had yet arrived.

Aaron looked around with appreciation for

the elegant comfort here. 'Did Hob build this?'

'No, but I think he might as well have. He remodelled it.

'Nearer his heart's desire?'

David winced.

Aaron took the glass and sipped. 'How is the boy?'

David sat down. 'I meant this to be social,' he said, 'with your family away. I hadn't realised that Abby had already asked the neighbours. Although that may be just as well.'

'Why?'

'I don't . . .' David changed his mind. 'I was going to say that I don't want to bother you. Fact is, I don't mind bothering you or anybody, if I could get some clue . . .'

'I can be as curious as the next man, too,' said Aaron.

So David glanced towards the opening into the stair-hall. Nobody was out there. 'We have had an announcement,' he said quietly. 'Ladd tore up that cheque. He tells us that he will not complete his college courses. He tells us that he will "come into Cunningham Company" on November twenty-sixth.'

'Chooses one, eh? Gives himself a considerable hiatus.' Aaron missed the point.

David twirled his glass. They could hear feet scraping on the brick of the terrace to which a glass panel was open. But the boys came into the house by the stair-hall and then a vibration that was not quite sound followed their feet up

44

the stairs.

'Who is the other one? The neighbour?'

'Well, that's Gary Fenwick,' said David. 'He is a neighbour, yes. Ladd's childhood chum.'

'Childhood?'

'Yes, you could call him Ladd's—I think "henchman" is the word.'

'There is a henchman temperament.' Aaron smiled. 'Just as there is the temperament that requires a henchman. I understood you to say "Lorimer".'

'Yes, it's Justin Lorimer who is off to Palo Alto tonight. A no-nonsense young fellow. I'm partial to Justin.'

'Ladd couldn't be jealous?'

'Oh, lord! No!' said David, startled. 'They are ships that pass, those two. And the little sister just tags along.

It's their father, Rafe, who's the old friend of the family.'

'What troubles you?' asked Aaron, in a moment.

'You didn't take note of the date, did you?'

'Date?'

'Ladd tells us that he will come into Cunningham Company on November twenty-sixth.'

'Just like that? You are quoting?'

'The date. That is the day Hob died.'

'Hmm.' Aaron pursed his mouth. 'I'd agree that it means *something*.'

'I may as well tell you that I'm a little

scared,' said David.

'Do you mean that? Why?'

'Maybe you'll see.'

'I assume you've tried talking things out.'

'Tried, indeed. Can't even get started.'

'Has his mother talked to him at all?'

'No, I don't think she has. Not specifically about his attitude towards me. Abby is troubled, I'm sure. But she and I can't discuss it too well. I'm on a kind of spot here, Aaron.'

'Yes, so I imagine.'

'Abby is, too, of course. It's Abby that I care about. If it weren't for her, I'd tackle the boy my own way. I'd do differently, I think. What I'm sure of . . . he needs somebody.'

'Is there some mentor that the boy has known well? A teacher?'

'If so, not here. Maybe at college. Although I doubt it.'

'There isn't a pastor?'

'A . . .?' It took David's mind a second to recognise the word. 'No,' he said sadly, 'nobody goes to church. At least, not these days.'

'A family doctor, then?'

'Ladd hasn't been to any doctor since I've been around. Abby has a doctor, very good with women over forty.' David looked into his empty glass. How little he knew about his stepson. Whether the boy had ever been to church in his life, for instance. To his own children, he had so many clues. The

46

experiences they'd had, their training, the questions they had asked and at least some of the answers they'd been given, the whole matrix of their adult minds. But to this boy, no clues. Except an old acquaintance with his parents and a great gap in that—all the years of the boy.

'How about this henchman?' Aaron was asking. 'What about him?'

'Can he be talked to? Would he feel concern? Would he be intelligent enough . . . ?'

'You'll meet him,' David said drearily.

'Loyal, of course. No good. How about Lorimer? The elder, the old friend of the family?'

David said, 'See what you think' in the same hopelessness.

'Sounds like a pretty complete isolation.'

'Is that peculiar?'

'No, unfortunately. There is a schism between the generations, worse than ever. Kids don't grow up in the same household with grandparents or uncles or aunts or poor relations or any elders that would be easier to relate to . . . just *because* they are less important . . . than the parents.'

'How do you get at him, then?' David demanded. 'Is Abby the only one?'

'Abby could be the worst one, last one.'

'Then what is done in other such instances?' David now insisted. 'When a boy is obviously . . .'

'Disturbed? Yes, well . . . if and when,' said Aaron, 'he falls ill to the point of showing crippling symptoms, or, if and when he does something that comes under the law . . .'

'In other words, nothing can be done until it is too late!' said David, rather angrily.

'You should try any approach.'

'I will. If I hear of any,' said David irritably. 'Something's happened. Something's hit him. Something's changed. Now he is decisive.'

'And that may be very hopeful.' said Aaron soothingly. 'Not every emotional problem leads to illness. On the other hand, it is true that some illnesses must get worse before they can be treated.'

'As a businessman,' said David crisply, 'that sounds to me like a hell of a note.'

'Perhaps it is,' said Dr. Silver.

* * *

Abby came in. 'Oh, good, you've given him a drink, David. Aaron, I can't tell you how nice it is to see you after so many years. Oh, please, sit down.'

She herself sank gracefully into a chair, her black chiffon dinner dress keeping its elegant lines. The flesh of her neck and shoulders showed sweetly through the veiling cloth that came demurely up to her pearl collar. A darling woman!

'This is going to be,' she said, 'the most

48

difficult table! We have six gentlemen and only two ladies. I do not know that Emily Post would have survived.' Abby mocked at her own exaggeration with her worried forehead and her mischievous eyes. David was offering her a cocktail with a twitching of his brows. 'No, thank you, dear. I'll just wait. I hope you can put up with us, Aaron. You see, Justin leaves tonight.'

'Doesn't your guest of honour have a lady friend?' inquired Aaron.

'Their name is legion,' said David. 'Our Justin can't award any one of them a prize like dinner *en famille*. Destroy his clever footwork on the tightrope.'

'He is an awfully nice boy,' said Abby. A shade of trouble crossed her smiling face. 'And, of course, it wouldn't have done to ask some girls just for the other boys.'

'I think we should have asked a bevy,' said David, 'and watched the fun. Ah, company's coming.'

Abby rose, excusing herself to Aaron. David went beside her to greet their guests. He thought, this is right. Abby and I. Why should I sit alone, a man made solitary by a loss? And why should Abby walk alone, when she need not? Because a child feels unhappy? He doesn't like his pattern changed? This child, who might just as well be thanking his stars that he is free. Are we taking him too seriously? Do we indulge him, even to think of his unhappiness as if it might be a disease? Was there ever man or woman who lived a life and has not met and survived some unhappiness? Where are we going with this theory that he may be ill? Abby and I are a fact of life. Ah yes, he thought, and so is thunder. If there is thunder and the baby cries you cannot stop the thunder. You wish to comfort the baby. But you had better not try to do it by saying that the thunder isn't there. The baby must be reconciled. Taught, he thought. But, for teaching, it is very late. This baby is twenty.

CHAPTER FOUR

It was a difficult table. Abby had done the best that could be done with it.

The preliminaries had not been too difficult. Rafe, innocently garrulous, had been very helpful. Justin had pinned Dr. Silver to a sofa with his candid, dark blue gaze and asked with unabashed curiosity for information about Aaron's profession. David had smiled to himself to see Aaron sparking up and responding to this lad's cool bright force.

Felicia, in sea-green, mousy as ever, had ventured a few remarks to Gary, who lapped up cocktails with an air of having fallen in a pleasant place where he felt nothing much was required of him.

50

During the preliminaries, it had not mattered that Ladd—immaculate, even foppish, in a dark suit—had wrapped himself in silence and mystery, volunteering nothing to anyone.

Now they were gathered to the table. Abby had put Dr. Silver to her left and Rafe to her right. Well, she couldn't have given Aaron to David and David was glad not to have Rafe. So, good enough.

She had put Felicia in the middle of one side, between Dr. Silver and Gary Fenwick, directly opposite Ladd, who, in the middle of the other side, was between Rafe and Justin. Very good, thought David. No father beside his son. No brother beside his sister. No husband beside his wife.

But this left David the prey of Justin's force, and David found himself having to hold back, remember his role, take care not to be carried away into a lively private conversation with the boy who wanted to know about Cunningham Company, and business in general, and asked some very provocative questions.

The arrangement also brought Aaron into the range of Rafe's chatter. Aaron, however, slipped out to say a few words to Felicia, now and again, to which the girl responded shyly. As for Gary, he ate what was put before him with silent relish, expecting neither to have to entertain or be entertained.

But Ladd . . .

Ladd, locked between Lorimers, sat silent.

Rafe threw a rhetorical question his way once in a while but expected and got no answer. Justin paid no attention to Ladd at all. And Ladd resisted David's few efforts to draw him into the discussion of Cunningham Company. So Ladd sat silent, wrapped in a private mysterious place of his own. He did not eat heartily, but rather with a pickiness that verged upon insult. Now and then he lifted white lids to glance at Aaron, at David, and then let white lids down with an effect of secrecy and craftiness. He was behaving like an actor. He seemed to think there was a spotlight, that he had everyone's attention.

And so he has, thought David. A good deal of his mother's attention, although Abby was skilful not to show it. And David's now. And surely, Dr. Silver's. And obviously Felicia's, since she had no skill to hide her quick glances. And even Gary's attention, what there was of it.

At last, the dark force in Ladd grated upon the bright force in Justin, and Justin turned and said cheerily, 'You're full of jokes tonight, old boy? Feel like changing your mind? I'll race you up there. You take the high road and I'll take the low road. What say?' Justin's manner had changed. There was just a trace of jolly condescension, as if he now spoke to a boy, not a man.

Ladd said with a lowering look, 'I have better things to do than play games.' There was a silence.

Then Felicia lifted her young voice. 'Did you ever get the Mozart, Ladd? The one you wanted?' (Good girl, thought David.)

Ladd answered with effort, but pleasantly enough, 'No, I never did. I forgot, actually.'

Dr. Silver said, 'You're fond of Mozart, are you?'

Ladd looked at him and said quickly and coldly, 'Now, what possible difference can it make to you whether I am fond of Mozart or not?'

David could feel Abby's pang. Abby could forgive anything better than bad manners. Such a piece of rudeness as this would be devastating to her. So David jumped, protectively, to speak before two seconds had ticked by. 'If people did not inquire about tastes and did not tell, each his own, I should say that ninety-five per cent of the conversation on this earth would not take place.' He spoke as genially as he could, trying for an air of amusement. 'Check on it. "I like summer." "I don't like cold weather." "I'm fond of salads." "Blue's my favourite colour." And the other fellow says, "Oh, I can't stand the heat." Or "Give me meat and potatoes." The strange thing is, that they both seem to be well satisfied with this exchange.' He was trying to bring a specific within an abstraction and so lead them away from an ugly moment. He wasn't sure how he was doing. 'Why is

53

that?' he inquired.

It was Felicia who had been following and who took up his challenge. 'Isn't it just a way to tell the kind of person you are?' She looked frightened at having thrown off mousehood.

'Is it, Doctor?' Ladd snapped, bending forward and somehow glittering with antagonism.

'I should think so. Wouldn't you?' Aaron smiled.

'So you don't care so much about Mozart? You just want to know the kind of person I am? At the dinner table?' Ladd's face looked a yellowish beige. He was pale under his tan. Abby's hand clutched for the table's edge. Rafe had his chin pulled in. He was lost. Justin was still as a cat. Gary chewed.

Aaron said calmly, 'Ah, but I do care about Mozart. It's nice to meet a fellow enthusiast. Are you one, Miss Felicia?'

Oh, nicely done, thought David. Now, let the brat shut up. It's his last chance.

Felicia said, with a shaky smile, 'There aren't many kinds of music that I *don't* like.'

'And what does that make *her*, Doctor?' said Ladd harshly.

David saw Abby's hand relax suddenly.

'That makes her,' said Aaron without much delay, 'a very pleasing young lady to sit next to at a dinner table.'

Pinked? Or not? No matter. David was not concerned for Dr. Silver, who could not be

54

insulted. The mere attempt would interest him professionally. David was worried for Abby and he damned the brat's selfish little soul and he spoke, coldly. 'It is considered courteous to answer a friendly question, Ladd. At the dinner table or anywhere else.' He took authority. He admonished, like a father.

The boy looked at him. The dark eyes glittered with outrage. David met the eyes. 'I apologise for you,' he went on deliberately, 'to your hostess and her guests.' He meant to cut. Now he expected an explosion. He wanted it, waited, braced for it. The boy looked as if he could fly apart, as if he only paused to let one wild word take precedence over another.

Then Abigail . . . Abigail . . . with her soft face strangely cool-looking, inclined her head and spoke to her son. 'Ladd?' The boy's head jerked. 'If you would like to be excused, dear,' said Abby gently, 'you may leave the table.'

The boy was absolutely still for one second. His face was narrowing, narrowing in, lids pulling, mouth tightening. Then his chair rasped on the carpet. He got up, tall and taut.

'Thank you, Mother,' he said, matching her gentleness with mocking melody. His eye had an animal knowledge. He was like someone stabbed but not yet bleeding. Numb before promised pain.

He marched to the hall. He went out of the house, upon the terrace, into summer darkness.

Abigail said, her lips trembling, eyes pleading. 'Please forgive him, everyone.' Her eyes evaded David's. She rang her little bell. She said, 'Justin, I know you must get off soon. But you will take time for dessert and coffee?'

'Sure will,' said Justin.

'Why do you drive at night, dear?' Abby was stating her wish. Talk, everyone.

So David said to Gary, 'What are *you* studying, these days?'

And Rafe said to Dr. Silver, 'I paint. I carve. I write a little poetry. But music means very little to me. Why is that?'

Cleona came in for the dinner plates.

*   *   *

Felicia's back was to the windows. She could feel Ladd out there. Watching, was he? No, please don't let him be watching this dinner party just go on, or know that talk, talk, talk was flowing and covering his empty place and filling it in, as water on the beach obliterates the print of your foot, as if you had never been there.

Oh, why did they all have to pretend that nothing had happened? Or else that something unpleasant had happened and therefore and only therefore should be ignored? Didn't they know what had happened?

Well, but poor Abby was upset and so they

were all thinking about poor Abby, now. Even Justin, who was carrying on about how the traffic was less and he could make time and he was going to stop off at a fellow's house in Los Gatos for breakfast. Then Dr. Silver was drawing Abby into some talk about music, shutting Rafe up and making her answer.

And Felicia refused the communication of her brother's eye.

Gary was telling David Crown that he was a Phys Ed major and wanted to be a coach but small colleges didn't get into big-time competition. But Felicia knew that David Crown was only half listening. *He* was worrying about Abby. His nice face—because she did think he was nice-looking—oh, it kept its quiet watch. He wasn't a strong and thunderous person like Mr. Cunningham had been. Of course, he wasn't exactly an old pussycat, either. Felicia didn't know him very well. She didn't know whether he had done what Ladd thought.

Didn't they know what Ladd thought?

Why did this have to be? Ice-cream and cake, in candlelight, and talk, talk . . . Why must Abby have a nice orderly dinner party as if *that* were the most important thing in the whole world? Why didn't any of them get up and go out there and find Ladd and try to tell him . . .

Tell him it wasn't true. That Dr. Silver hadn't been asked here to spy on him, to find out whether Ladd was mentally ill and needed a doctor (just because he couldn't feel happy about a pretty sudden stepfather)! Or . . . if it was true and David Crown had done this, then couldn't someone tell Ladd that it was only because they worried about him? Make him believe it? Oh, comfort him. Surely he was more important than a stupid party.

Couldn't any of them tell what had been bothering Ladd all evening? The headshrinker, of course. And it was a little bit funny. Dr. Silver didn't really fit into this particular party.

Felicia did not know the truth about that, but she wished she, herself, had the courage to get up and go out there and find him. But she hadn't. Because of Rafe, who would then certainly come down with his heavy hand. Or because of Justin, who had warned her off, who might follow her and argue. Felicia cringed in herself.

Or because she had really no status, just her secret devotion and her strong wish to comfort him, somehow. Look at his own mother, who had the status and the right. *She* wasn't doing a single thing but being upset and requiring everybody else to comfort *her.*

Then Dr. Silver said in Felicia's ear, softly, 'Are you all right?'

And she cringed. But she answered softly, 'You talk to poor Abby.'

Then she knew he had read her, she knew

he saw right through to her feeling about Abby, and everything. These doctors were spooky. Horrible. Felicia didn't blame Ladd. She didn't blame him at all. They were intrusive. They didn't let you *alone.* You had a right to feel what you *did* feel and a right not to have to tell anybody what that was, if you'd rather not.

You even had a right to be unhappy. It was just phony to try to tell yourself that everything was really rosy. That all you had to do was change your attitude . . . put on the old rose-coloured glasses . . . that would fix everything. Well, it wouldn't.

There are worse things, she thought, than being rude because you feel spied on and betrayed, when maybe you are. There is something basically wrong and unrosy. Because look . . . she reasoned with herself . . . probably all these people are, right now, trying to be good and kind, all helping Abby pretend because they think that's right. They are not doing it to be mean or anything. And yet . . .

Felicia herself was being a 'good girl,' eating her ice-cream daintily and not bothering anybody.

And yet . . .

Maybe it isn't good enough, just to be 'good.' Maybe it's just not that easy.

Of course not. Of course not. The secret made her smile.

The night was cool. The moon was not up. Felicia had hold of Justin's hard arm, because of her high heels and the dark, but the Lorimers knew the Cunningham grounds almost as well as their own. So they crossed the terrace and took the walk to the steps, to the driveway.

Justin didn't say a word.

*   *   *

It had been quite simple for Felicia to get away, after dinner. There had been the milling around in the Cunningham stair-hall, everybody saying 'Good-bye,' 'Good luck.' Then Abby had taken Gary Fenwick by his arm and on into the living-room. Dr. Silver had followed them.

Rafe had gone into his annual speech to his departing son. It was always the same—on the importance of human values over against materialism, friendships and all that, but of course your friends might as well be high-class well-heeled people. On getting along with others as a sign of maturity, but of course you must always 'be yourself.' A speech full of paradox. Justin always listened to it quietly, with his face closed, patient. Then he would go away and do as he would do, which would be very well.

60

When Rafe ran down, Felicia was able to say to her father, 'Dad, why don't I walk over with Justin and see him off? You stay at the party.'

Rafe had been just as pleased to stay. David Crown, waiting politely, had said to her, 'But you'll come back, won't you, Felicia?'

'Oh, yes, Mr. Crown,' she had said, 'of course.'

*　　*　　*

Justin, once they had achieved the level of the drive-way, disengaged his arm and crossed to try the pool gate. It was locked.

'We locked it this afternoon,' Felicia said.

'I know.' He peered within where the pool glimmered faintly. He turned—she could see him now by starlight or by the city's sky-reflected glow—and started along the drive towards the gap in the high hedge by which opening the Lorimers came and went. She followed.

'His car is here,' Justin said, as they passed the Cunningham garage and carport. Her heart jumped. She had not heard Ladd's car go out, but then she might not have been able. So it was here. 'I'm wondering where he got to,' said her brother. 'What an idiot!' They went through the gap.

Justin's car, which was five years old but well-kept and spry with power—since Justin

61

understood machinery in the way he had of effortlessly knowing what he cared to know— was waiting in the Lorimers' drive. Justin, being Justin, had already stashed his stuff in trunk and tonneau. He stopped and looked up at their house. The clap-boards that were greying by daylight, rose up whitely now. A light burned in the kitchen. The doors were never locked. (It was Rafe's philosophy.) This was the house where they had been born. Felicia knew no other place.

'Well,' said Justin, 'so . . .' He seemed to try to shrug off house, town, family. He got into his car. He started the engine and listened to it purr.

Felicia moved closer. 'Have fun,' she said.

'Oh, sure.'

But there was more to be said; it hung heavy in the air.

'I suppose,' her brother said, 'your heart bleeds for poor Ladd Cunningham. You should try your brain.'

'Don't you know it was that doctor?' Felicia almost whispered, as if the night listened. 'Don't you see what Ladd thought? Well, it's terrible, and somebody should try to talk to him and let *him* talk. Somebody is going to have to.'

Her brother turned on his headlights and the dashlight came up to play upon his face. 'I suppose you're going to volunteer and make a damned fool of yourself. *Qué sera sera*, eh?

You're an idiot.'

'Thanks a *lot*,' she said, stepping back.

Justin was peering along the headlight's beam. The light touched their father's studio, the big tree, the bench, the hedge, a patch of whiteness, beyond the gap that was the Cunningham's pavement. All things looked strange, tonight, around this place where they had been born.

'Next year,' said Justin flatly, 'you can get away.'

'What if I don't want . . . ?'

'You don't know what you want.'

'But you do?'

'Oh, I'll get it,' he said, misunderstanding her. 'Just don't make people up, huh, Felice?'

'What?'

'Don't invent them, I mean. They're sitting there. *Out* there.'

'All those idiots?' Felicia said thinly. 'Really?'

'Okay.' Justin seldom bothered to take offence and did not, now. 'I kinda wish I didn't have to go,' he said, 'but . . . *qué sera.* So long, honey.' Whereupon he put his car in gear and backed, with his usual verve, towards the street and away.

His sister stood in the tweedy duskiness of the suburban night. She felt her heart ache. Her brother never called her 'honey.' It was odd. For a moment, she mourned his departure. He was himself. A rare bird!

63

She had a feeling that it was not so much that he had gone. (He was himself.) He had let her go.

Now the days would settle to Rafe and Felicia, in the big old house, with Mrs. Wells, the cleaning woman, twice a week.

And Ladd Cunningham around.

* * *

Felicia shivered and turned her back upon the walls of home so whitely high.

Where *had* he got to?

She went through the gap. Her heels clicked on the pavement. She did not want to go back to the party. Where would Ladd be? Not at Gary Fenwick's house. Gary was still trapped in the party. Was he within the pool's fence, sitting somewhere in shadow? Was he in the garden, that square of shrubs and roses inside the wall? Her heels clicked.

She passed the carport, just a roof over Ladd's car, an afterthought, squeezed between garage and hedge. The big three-place garage was open. The Cunninghams . . . she really ought to get used to saying the Crowns . . . rarely pulled the doors down. Abby's car, David Crown's car. The car nearest the garden end. Hob Cunningham's car. She looked at it, hard. The parachute cloth was altered from its normal position. Then she knew where he was!

'Ladd?' But in her mind lingered a thought

about her brother. Justin thinks he is so smart!
He missed it! Hah! The heart's a better
compass than the brain!

*   *   *

In the big living-room, Abby was busily
charming Gary Fenwick—an evasion, a
desperate ploy.

Rafe had undertaken to explain to Dr.
Silver some basic insights into human
motivations. But Aaron, at the first decently
possible moment, arose and said that he must
go. So, this having been politely regretted but,
as politely, not disputed, he went, and David
accompanied him to his car which he had left
in the street.

'Not me,' said Aaron. 'Out. Out. Surely,
that's obvious?'

'Yes, I suppose so. Where is he, I wonder?'

'Beer parlour? Cathouse? Wild drive into
the country? Or,' said Aaron reflectively,
'possibly he's got in, secretly, and lies on his
bed, which might be unfortunate.'

'What will happen?'

'I don't know.'

'What am I going to do?' David was not
asking for answers, not from Aaron but from
the universe.

'To protect Abby?'

'Yes. No. I don't know.'

Aaron said, 'It could be . . . and I suppose

65

I'd better say so . . .'

'Yes?'

'That what he hates is himself, that he is trying to take you for himself, that he might fail. If so—then, you had better take care for Abby.'

'I don't . . .'

'Ah, well, I don't either. Nor can I. Out. Out. And much the better part of valour. I'll have to leave you with it.'

He got into his car. 'I'm sorry, Dave,' he said. And David knew that his friend was sorry.

*　　　*　　　*

He stood alone on the sidewalk in front of Hob Cunningham's house. Damn the Greeks, he thought, and their word for it. Oh cruel! You could not . . . could not . . . (How could you?) . . . if you loved and proposed to protect a sensitive woman, tell her that her son was sick of incestuous love for her. When she, according to her instincts, according to her best, had only and only loved her son as God gives a woman to do.

No, said David to himself. No and no!

My daughters, he thought, loved me and yet now love their husbands and, as far as I can know or tell, they do so safely. And surely not because *I* was too wise to love them, only and only, as God gives a man to love his daughters.

66

Oh cruel doctrine and bitter punishment and mockery! If God is love but love is *evil* . . .

He went up the walk to the house feeling frightened and lost. He went into the stair-hall where the lovely curve of the stairs flew up, where subtly upon the air hung the remembrance of good food, where faintly to be heard came the sound of human voices. He went into a human habitation.

So David drew himself into himself. Being human, he loved. 'Though He slay me yet will I trust in Him. But I will maintain my own ways before Him.'

Now how had that popped into his head, complete? Job? Yes, he knew it was from Job, and knew not how he knew. He was no Bible student. Ah, thought David, it would be my father or my mother who would remember how I come to know those words. Love sounded down his years, behind him.

Feeling strong and resettled upon his foundations, he went towards the voices.

*   *   *

'Don't touch it!' Ladd said fiercely. Felicia had taken steps towards the garage. He got out of his father's car where he had been sitting in the driver's seat, and slammed the door, and pulled the cover over the hood. He hurried out to her. He did not touch her but they walked a step or two together as if he were leading her,

67

by suggestion, away.

'I'm so glad I found you,' she said. 'Let's . . . let's go somewhere.'

She was wondering where they could go to talk. Not into the garden or anywhere too near the Cunningham house. Not the pool house either, because that involved getting the gate key from its hiding place and unlocking. Too formal and deliberate a course. No, quickly— where? Then she thought of the wooden bench against her father's workroom, under the camphor tree.

'I know,' she said. 'Please, Ladd . . . come with me. This way.'

His feet scuffed the pavement as he walked with her. They went through the gap in the hedge. Felicia was very happy. 'No one will know,' she murmured, thinking that they would be lost from all interference in the strangeness of this very familiar place. She reached for his hand to draw him towards the bench. But he snatched his hand away. He was looking up at the Lorimer house.

'Justin just left,' she said reassuringly. 'There's nobody home.'

'What do you want?'

'Just . . . please, Ladd? I know . . . I mean . . . the way you felt. I mean, I think I do.' Felicia was very young. Her speaking vocabulary sometimes failed to match up to her inner musings. She stammered. 'I mean, I wish I could . . . you know? Please, let me?'

68

She could not see him very well. The dusk concealed expression. She was yearning to read the blank oval of his face. She would comfort. She would save. She, Felicia. Poised upon a sense of heavenly power, she did not feel her feet upon the earth. She was disembodied.

So his hard fingers shocked her when he took her by her shoulders and his hard mouth and cruel teeth and his kiss of anger. She was jolted back into her body by pain and surprise.

'Oh, you lousy bitches!' he said. 'Oh, she's a bird and you're a bird! Birds of prey! What? What? So we're supposed to go upstairs? Whose bed? Your bed? No one will know. I'm surprised you give a damn who knows. *She* doesn't.'

'Please . . .' Her voice was feeble. She felt as if she would faint. 'No.'

'Ah, come on,' he said with loathing. 'I'll tell you something, sister. None of that.' So his hands threw her and she fell hard and the ground was cruel but she began to whimper from a worse pain. 'Just figure that you didn't make it, honey,' Ladd said, a tall menace, a terror. She thought for a moment that he would pull back his foot and kick her. But he did not. He turned and went back through the hedge and when he melted in the dark, he laughed.

CHAPTER FIVE

When the phone rang, David answered. He came back into the big room and said, 'That was Felicia to say she isn't feeling awfully well.'

'Not?' said Rafe, looking startled.

'Begs to be excused, Abby. Thanks you for a lovely dinner.'

'Ah, poor child,' said Abby. 'What can be the matter?'

Rafe said, 'Perhaps I'd better go along home and see. No one's there, you know.'

Gary said, 'Yeah, me too. I mean, thanks a lot, Mrs. Crown, Mr. Crown, for everything.'

So the party was breaking up, at last.

Gary was younger, more spry, and had fewer phrases of farewell at his command, so he went first. Out upon the terrace, down to the driveway, to turn towards the Lorimers' gap because it was a short-cut for him to go that way. As he drew even with the pool gate he heard Ladd say from against the garden wall, 'Hey, Gare?'

'Hey, Ladd?'

'Listen, I think I know how to work what we said. Let's kick it around.'

'Well, sure.'

'Listen, let's *go*.'

'Okay. My place?'

'I got to get out of *this* God-damned, rotten,

stinking place. What took you?' Ladd snapped irritably.

'I had to be polite.'

They were moving fast. They were through the gap.

'Say, the head-doctor cut out, but quick,' Gary said. 'I guess he'd had it.' He stopped because suddenly he had gone ahead. 'You coming?'

Ladd was standing still in the Lorimers' yard and seemed to be looking at the ground.

'I'd just as soon cut out of the whole damn' stinking world,' Ladd said. 'And maybe that's the best idea of all.'

'Listen.'

But Ladd hurried on and Gary followed.

*　　*　　*

David and Abby were in their bedroom. They had left a door to the terrace open, not knowing whether the boy had his key. They had left a light in the stair-hall.

Abby sat down at her dressing-table and held her cheeks. 'But where is he?' she mourned.

'I don't know, darling. After all, he is twenty.' David sawed at his tie.

'But what was the matter with him? He surely knows better. David, what is it? I've done wrong. I must have done wrong.' She was weeping. 'Hob was always so busy. I had the

71

job of raising Ladd. I must not have done a very good job. I've never been so mortified. What will Aaron Silver think of us?'

David was not going to tell her all that Aaron Silver thought. 'Don't worry about him,' he counselled.

Abby held her cheeks and said to the mirror, 'Have I done wrong?'

David came to stand behind her and stroke her shoulders. 'I will not leave you,' he said, decisively.

Her startled eyes met his by way of the mirror.

'I've gone over that a thousand times. Abby darling, consider something. A parent is not supposed to own a child. A child is not a possession.'

'I know.'

'Then, neither does a child own a parent. Mustn't it work both ways?'

'But . . . Help me?' Her hands were frantic at the clasp of her pearl collar. David stepped back and bent to help her. 'But David,' Abby said in a moment, 'yes, he does, in a way.'

'When he was small? When you had to be sure he didn't kill himself, from ignorance? Then you were, in a sense, his slave and bodyguard.'

'Yes, I was.'

'But not now.'

'I didn't think so.'

'I won't leave you,' he repeated.

'I couldn't bear it if you did.' Her eyes were brimming. 'I suppose it's hard for him. That I have you, but he—still misses his father. Yet Hob didn't have time, you know.' Her eyes yawed, begging for comfort. Begging a place to put the blame? 'He left so much of the job to me. Hob was busy.'

David turned away and walked apart.

'Of course, I know he did it all for us,' she said.

'It's a superstition,' said David.

'What is?'

David jingled the change in his pocket. 'Abby, you are a beloved woman, but you are not responsible, all by yourself, for the whole world.'

'Poor world,' she said, 'if I were.'

'And neither was Hob.' (And neither am I.) David felt angry. 'Just don't fall for the guff they put out on the woman's club circuit. The cliché of the businessman father who is guilty: Guilty of what? Of being a man?'

He was thinking. Why should a man pretend to *be* a child, and play the games of childhood, if they bore him stiff? Let the little boy play games with his peers and test and affirm himself. Let the man go out, as the cave man went. Let him fight, in the market-place, the sabre-toothed tigers of our time. He meets what he has to meet and it isn't easy: Why should he be made to feel guilty for doing what he had better do—test and affirm his adult self?

He said aloud, 'Don't fall for the guff that implies he should do his man's work on the sly, bootleg it in, between Boy Scout meetings and visits to the zoo. *He* pays attention.'

Abby had stopped her tears. She was looking at him with her own mixed expression, part serious, part amused surprise.

'Attention to your child does not, believe me, equal time-spent-with,' said David. 'Attention happens to be a depth dimension, not span.'

He was thinking, And a man who loves his son does not throw sops, either. Not if he's honest. A man who loves his son will show him a man.

He said, 'And a mother does her son no favour to pretend that she is not also a woman.'

Abby loosened the top of her dress. A spark of mischief crossed her face. 'I'm not aware of having denied it.' Her hands still, she looked at herself in the glass.

David returned to stand at her back. His hands moved the fabric and caressed her bare shoulders. Her hands jumped to stop the motion of his. 'But where is he? Why did he behave the way he did tonight?'

'Oh, what way?' said David. 'He was rude. Well?' (He wanted to hurt someone, David was thinking, probably me. So he was rude to my friend.) He said aloud, 'We can make too much of it, Abby.'

'He *must* know better.'

'Well, then, he'll be sorry.'

Abby leaned back against him. 'He knows he was naughty,' she said sleepily. 'Oh, David, I do need you.'

Abby was comforted but David felt guilty. 'Naughty' was not the word for this boy's trouble. He felt, and almost for the first time, a true sympathy for the poor kid. With something of Hob in him and something of Abby, and something both more and less, new in the world since the dawn of time, unique— the blend of himself, unknown, unsorted yet. Poor suffering young person and his disease.

*　　　*　　　*

Rafe went home. He put up the hall light and turned off the light in the kitchen. He started up the stairs, that were steep and old-fashioned.

In the upper hall, he paused to collect his senses. Justin gone. His room now empty for the winter. Yes, silence there. No breathing boy. Rafe tiptoed to his own room and lit it, went back into the hall and towards the front of the house where Felicia was. He struck his knuckles lightly upon her door. 'Felicia, dear?'

'Dad?'

'Are you all right? May I come in?'

She stood, the other side of the wood, in her slip. Her sea-green dress was on a chair, badly stained and one sleeve torn. Her back was bruised. Her head hurt. Her right shoulder cap had been skinned. She had been trying to wash the dirt away from the abrasion.

'How do you feel, love?' her father said.

She felt so terrible that there was no name for it and no medicine. 'I'm all right,' she said, in as strong a voice as she could summon up. 'I'm just going to bed.'

'May I?'

'Please, Dad. I'm not ill. I'm tired.' She was desperate to save something. He must not know. He must not see.

'But what happened?' Rafe knew that the young were not tired for no reason.

'Daddy, I don't want to talk about it. I'm just a little bit upset because Ladd and I had a kind of quarrel, that's all.'

'Oh? He was waiting around for you, was he?'

She said 'I guess so' in a fainting voice. (Oh, please, let me alone. I can't tell you. You'll get all indignant and go blustering around and I don't want it known. It's bad enough . . . it's bad enough.) She said, 'I don't imagine we'll have anything more to do with each other. It's nothing to worry about. I want to go to sleep. I don't like having to be mean. Daddy, please?'

Rafe's face, in the hall, was shrewd and Felicia suddenly seemed to be able to see it through the wood. She knew the way his imagination was turning. She couldn't help it.

'Well, I'm sorry,' her father said. 'All right, darling. I think perhaps it's just as well and just as wise.' (He was not at all sorry. He was rather pleased.)

'I think so too,' said Felicia, in loud despair. 'Good night, Dad.'

'Good night, love.'

So Rafe made his way to his own bedchamber with a fond twist upon his lips. It did not cross his mind at first that the 'quarrel' had been anything but verbal. Well, his intuition had made the diagnosis days ago. Ladd was painfully in love. Hmm. But Felicia, it seemed, did not want him for a suitor. Well! And just as well. For one thing, they were cousins. Oh, remote. Rafe himself was a distant cousin to Abigail Ladd. Rafe thought, But that is a point. Perhaps if it were to be explained to the boy, gently. He thinks his heart is broken. If he got up his nerve, in spite of his mother—Abby would not have liked it. That was a part of the poor boy's trouble, of course. Neither would I like it, Rafe resolved. He must be a poor thing to have got himself into such a state over a puppy sort of love. Twenty and seventeen. Rafe sighed. He remembered his own youth and its innocence and turmoil. But Felicia, his little girl, must *not* be bothered or upset. Not any more. She was too young, too young for the problems of the flesh. Oh, Rafe knew about them. And that was it! *Now*, his intuition told him. Well, no

77

more of that!

He undressed and climbed into his lonely bed where (the fact was) had his wife Sylvia miraculously appeared, in her flesh, Rafe would have been perfectly miserable and very much frightened.

In her darkened room, Felicia crept under her blanket. She buried her head but could not cry. You are supposed to understand and to forgive. But she was beaten and sick at heart, having ridden, for a brief moment, on wings, fancying herself perfect in loving goodness . . . whence she had been dashed down into hell.

*   *   *

They were sitting on an old-fashioned lawn swing in the Fenwick's backyard. Gary did the yard work here, since his folks both went to business. He clipped and he mowed, but he never bothered to move the swing, so tall weeds had grown up through the slats of the footpiece. The tall stiff grasses could be annoying, so Ladd was cross-legged on one slatted seat and Gary cross-legged upon the other. They kept their voices low, although there was no one to hear them. The neighbourhood was abed.

'You're sure he is coming to Sunday dinner? Tomorrow?'

'Well, he's invited,' Gary said. 'My mom thinks her brother never gets a decent meal, so she pretty near always does invite him. He'll show up, okay. He pretty near always does. Unless—I mean, the Police Department—sometimes they get emergencies.'

'Nothing we can do about that,' said Ladd with a brisk and intelligent effect, 'But your uncle is pretty high brass, right?'

'Well, he is supposed to be second in command in the Detective Bureau. He's been there—'

'Yes, but what I want to know . . . Now wait, let me lay this out. I call up and ask for Walter Douglas. Then I tell him—'

'What are you going to tell him?'

'I'm going to give him an anonymous tip-off. Don't worry. He won't know who's calling.'

'Yes, but I don't know if I get it, Ladd,' said Gary. 'I mean, the point.'

'Listen, sure you do. But what I want to know, now—Will your uncle just amble into headquarters like, say, on Monday morning and report the call? Or, will he start investigating on his own, right away?'

'I don't know,' said Gary dully.

'All right then, I'm going to tell you what you've got to do.'

'Me?'

'Right. What I want is for your uncle to come to my house on Sunday afternoon, when dear David is there and I am there to watch him get the news.'

'Huh?'

'When he finds out that the police have had a tip, he's got to react. Can't you see that I have got to be there, watching him? So your uncle has got to come over.' Ladd felt clear-headed and ready for intricate planning, for the use of the power of the sly and cunning brain. Oh, he saw everything very clearly and he would cause these puppets all to dance.

'Uncle Walt might start checking around,' said Gary, 'but I don't know if he'd come over. I mean, he'd check around for evidence.'

'There's more than one kind of evidence.'

'What d'you expect David to do?'

'I don't know, but whatever he does, then I'll know.' A shaft of darkness, unexpected and uncontrollable, cut his inner light. 'And so will my mother, if she doesn't know already.'

'I still don't see . . . Hey, your dad had cancer, didn't he?'

'They could have waited,' said Ladd and his voice was flat, unresonant. 'Mercy is one thing. But if they couldn't wait to get to bed—' He hadn't meant to say that. He went on, furiously, 'That's murder in my book. And in your uncle's, too, if you want to know. That happens to be against the law.'

'Uncle Walt knows the law. And what to do,' said Gary, a trifle sulkily.

'He's going to do what I want him to do. And you are going to make him do it.' Ladd's temper had slipped. He caught for bright reason. 'What time do you have dinner?'

'On Sunday? Oh, around one. One o'clock.'

'What time will he get there?'

'Oh, twelve-thirty. Or quarter-to. After church.'

'He goes to *church*!'

'Yeah, he does,' said Gary apologetically.

'Okay,' said Ladd impatiently. 'How long does dinner take?'

'I dunno. Say till two o'clock, maybe?'

'Then what?'

'Then? Well, Uncle Walt's not married, so he usually kinda hangs around. He and my dad go in the den. If there's a ball game on, they watch. Or maybe they play gin. He hangs around. Sometimes he even stays for supper.

'Right after dinner is the time.'

'Why?'

'Because your mom isn't going to let him out of the house before he eats. You know that.'

'Sure do.'

'So—The phone's in the den? Right?'

'Yeah—the downstairs phone.'

'So we'll synchronise our watches, like they say, and right on the dot of two-thirty you go in there and you start as if to use the phone. As if you're going to call me, for instance. What's up? And all that.'

'Okay.'

'If everything is set on my end, if they haven't gone out or got company, I mean, then I'll ask for Walter Douglas. So you call him to

81

the phone.'

'Okay. What if he doesn't come tomorrow?'

'Then you tell me that, stupid! Now, if he is there, and he takes the call, you stand right by the phone. Because you are supposed to be wanting to use it as soon as he hangs up.'

'Sure.'

'Now, when he does hang up, or I do— Maybe you're going to have to put on a little act, Gare.'

'I dunno.'

'I'm going to tell you exactly what to do.'

'Okay. What?'

'Pretend you could hear the name Cunningham. Maybe you pretend you could hear the whole thing. So you say . . . "Hey, I know the Cunninghams. Ladd Cunningham is my best friend," you say. "What's all this?" you say.'

'Well, Uncle Walt though . . . he doesn't talk too much about police business.'

'That's why you're going to be right there, pretending you heard it. So he won't have to tell you. So then you say that the Cunninghams live only two blocks away.'

'Yeah.'

'And you ask him what he's going to do. Is he going to the Cunninghams?'

'And what if he says he's not going to do anything?' said Gary, in sudden rebellion.

'Okay,' said Ladd. 'Maybe so. But that's when you've got to say that you're going right

82

over to tell us about it. And you just do that. You do that, Gare. You go over to my house and you say there's been this phone call. And if dear David doesn't want to believe it, he can check with your uncle. Your uncle is going to have to say yes, he got the call. So it will work out, either way. Neat?'

Gary said nothing.

Ladd said, 'It's not too tough, to put on an act. All you have to do is think to yourself what you would do "if." Just put it out of your mind that you know who's calling. Just think what you would do if you happened to be standing there, and somebody was telling your uncle that Hob Cunningham was murdered.'

'Yeah,' said Gary with sudden enlightenment.

'All right. You'd tell your uncle that you knew us. You'd ask him what he was going to do. You'd come barrelling over to tell *me*.'

'Sure.'

Ladd brooded. 'It would be better, though, if your uncle came himself.'

Gary said, 'What if the line is busy?'

'What? Your line? My line? I'll just call the first second that I can, after two-thirty.' Ladd felt there was nothing he could not explain. 'Anything else bother you?'

Gary said, 'It might cause a lot of trouble. You know that.'

'I know that,' Ladd said impatiently and then in a moment, 'What's the matter?'

Gary said, 'I don't know if you know this.

83

They could get an exhumation order. Uncle Walt did that, one time. I remember, it turned out suicide.'

Ladd sat still as stone. He was frightened. Dark shafts danced. Then he said, 'My father never quit. He never did. He never would. I saw him on Thanksgiving. He told me. "You've got to stick it out, the whole way," he said, "and that's all there is to it. It's that simple," he said to me.' Ladd put his head down and began to mutter rapidly. 'Listen you can laugh. The whole rotten world can laugh. Maybe there isn't anybody who wouldn't laugh. Because it *is* pretty simple. If I opened my stupid mouth and said the word, you wouldn't know what I was talking about. I'd be a fool to open my mouth . . .'

Gary, a lap or two behind, said, 'He had guts, eh?'

Ladd bent over. 'That, too.'

'I liked him real well.'

'You saw him about twice in your whole life,' snarled Ladd.

'What's the difference?' Gary said. 'And I saw him more than that. You forget.'

But Ladd, who could not forget, or totally remember, now wept in silence for his father. Whom he had failed. Wept for his failure. When he had flown back to school that Thanksgiving night, putting away from him hard thoughts of death, of pain, and (what was even harder to bear) thoughts of courage. Or

84

guts. Or *honour*! The plane had been full of young people. They would have laughed. Oh, not because his Dad was dying, but because— you didn't even use a word like 'courage'. You said 'guts.' You did not say '*honour.*' Ever. Yes, but . . . but . . . but . . . but—He shook out of chaos to remembrance.

So the next day, back to classes, the jolly old routine. Not for one moment (while he wept— cross-legged in the swing, in the night— remembering) did he allow himself to remember plain the brief lightness that had come to him when, knowing that his father was going to die, he had gone off, laughing. No, what he writhed for was remorse. Remorse, of course, a horse, of course, remorse. He hadn't paid enough attention. Oh, not that he hadn't just sat there by the hospital bed. It was that he had not thought enough about his father. Or his mother. Or David Crown. But how could I have known? he asked himself, for comfort. I honestly didn't know. How vile! How rotten! They had no honour. They gave him no honour. They wouldn't even let him die, in his own way, his honourable death. And so I'll kill David Crown. He'll never die an honourable death in my mother's house, my father's bed. I'll kill him. I have to. Oh, he's a bird! A cuckoo bird, old David! Rotten and old and pretty sly . . . but a cuckoo bird and what is that? Oh, something, listen? I have to. Don't I?

85

Gary had been chewing on nothing, in his puzzled way. He spoke. 'Maybe you should've finished up at Stanford. I mean, didn't he say you should "stick it out"?'

Ladd unfolded and sprang up. 'Listen, you bastard, he was killed! And David Crown is lousy stinking murderer! And what do you want?'

'Nothing. I didn't say . . .'

'If you're not my buddy, buddy, then I'll get a gun some place—and don't think I can't. And I'll shoot dear David in his head and myself, too. I'd just as soon. It would be a lot simpler. You're the one keeps talking about evidence and this terrific uncle you've got in the police department.'

'I'm going to do what you want,' said Gary. 'Don't get so excited.'

CHAPTER SIX

Very early Sunday morning, David woke to catch Abby slipping quietly back into their room. 'He's asleep,' she said. 'He's home.'

*　　　*　　　*

They were having a late breakfast on the terrace, surrounded by the Sunday papers, when Ladd came out of the house in trunks, carrying a towel. His mien was bland, his eyes innocent.

'I'm sorry about last night, Mother. I hope it didn't spoil the party.' When they did not answer, he continued, 'I don't know why, but that Dr. Silver irritates me. I couldn't stand him. I know I should have kept still. *I'm* sorry.'

Now, into his blandness, there crept a slightly sullen note as if to say, You had better appreciate my handsome apology or *you* will be at fault, you know.

'Dear, I'm glad, said Abby, 'that you realise how much you embarrassed me. I knew that you *would*.' She was eager to forgive. She praised.

Ladd said to David, all meek and mild, 'I guess I owe you an apology, sir. I know you invited him here.'

David simply nodded, for under the humble pose now crept the antagonism.

Abby said, 'Well, we'll say no more about it, shall we? The next time Dr. Silver comes you'll be able to make your apologies to him, dear, and I'm sure he will accept them kindly. Swim before breakfast?' Thus Abby announced that all was now as well as could be.

Ladd struck at his bare leg with the towel. 'Cleona said she'd bring me a tray. Okay?' He seemed to be thinking over what had just been said.

David cleared his throat. 'Aaron Silver's family is flying home this evening. I shouldn't think we'll ever have them all to dinner.'

'You've never met his wife?' asked Abby, brightly.

'No, and the children are very young, I believe he said.'

He was dragging this in awkwardly, but David was sending a message. An explanation? Perhaps even an admission? Certainly a promise.

And the boy was reading all of it. His eyes turned uneasily. He seemed dismayed. 'You going to be around?' he said, rather awkwardly. 'Or is somebody coming over?'

'Not that I know,' his mother answered. 'We'll just be lazy.'

'Quiet Sunday at home,' said David.

The boy looked across the garden and his mouth threatened to smile. 'Well, here goes,' he said suddenly. And suddenly, he went.

David sipped cold coffee. The roses were beginning their fall bloom; the quiet Sunday air was sweetly fragrant. Peace lay on the pleasant garden scene. The clank and rattle of the board, the explosion of water as the boy dived, broke the silence pleasantly. David pondered; what was it that, for a moment, had dismayed him? It couldn't have been the message. (Aaron Silver. Out. Out.) Then what? To have been able to read my message? Did that give him a turn? What if he wants me to remain the enemy? But what if I broke through, just now, if only in the smallest way?

It must be harder to keep a man an enemy if you can communicate with him.

He felt happier. He had forgotten Aaron's enigmatic warning. He smiled at Abby. She looked happier, too.

*   *   *

Nobody came to swim. Not even Gary. There was no sign of either of the Lorimers. It was not the custom of the house to serve a large Sunday dinner in the middle of the day. Cleona went off duty. Abby would herself prepare them a hearty, but informal meal at suppertime. So it was a quiet Sunday at home.

Until three o'clock in the afternoon. David was in the room at the front of the house that Hob had called the 'den' but Abby called the 'library.' It was a bookish and leathery place that Hob had modelled after some masculine dream or other. In fact, it was Abby who used the room most. But David had fled the light. He'd had enough sunshine. He was peacefully reading when he heard voices. Then Abby came in, leading a stranger, after whom followed Ladd and Gary Fenwick.

'David, this is Mr. Douglas.'

'Mr. Douglas?'

'Gary's uncle.'

'Very pleased to meet Gary's uncle. How are *you*, Gary?'

'Fine,' said Gary mechanically.

There was something in the air.

'Will you sit down, Mr. Douglas? Or shall we all go into the other room?'

'Mr. Crown,' said Gary's uncle. He was a stocky man of middle age, obviously muscular. He was almost totally bald. The pink of his scalp was like a cap above the brown and weathered face. 'I'm in the Police Department. Detective Bureau.' His eyes were a pale, shiny, almost icy grey. He had a deep voice and it was, David realised, apologetic and conciliatory. 'I wonder if Mrs. Crown could let me speak to you privately for a minute.'

'What is it?' cried Abby instantly. If this man's purpose had been not to alarm her, he had accomplished the opposite.

'I don't think it's a thing,' said Gary's uncle. He understood, at once, that there was no putting Abby out. 'I've had a kind of funny phone call, ma'am. I guess you folks better know about it. Especially since Gary, here, was going to come over and tell you anyway.'

'Tell us what, please?' Abby had her hands clasped and held hard against her breast. David stood at her back, having been drawn there, irresistibly.

'It's nothing to upset you too much,' said Gary's uncle. 'Only some crackpot. This kind of thing happens. Whoever this nut is, he knew I was in the Department, you see?'

David said to his wife, 'Sit down, darling.' He put her gently into a leather chair. 'Sit

90

down, please,' he said to the others. 'Now, let's have it.'

He himself perched on the arm of Abby's chair. Something in the air. The two boys sat down, far to the left of David's field of vision.

'Well, it's not too pleasant, you know,' said Douglas. He had seated himself, but only on the chair's edge. He was supported on a firm tripod, his two feet and a minimum of his rump. 'It has to do with the late Mr. Cunningham.'

'With Hob?' Abby held her throat. David could feel the rhythm of her heartbeat. He slipped his arm down the chair back and rest his hand upon her far shoulder. 'A phone call?' he prompted.

'Well, you must know we do get this kind of thing. I am at my sister's for dinner and somebody wants me on the phone. Whoever it was knew where to find me, you see? Well, what he said to me, I think I'd better tell you, because you may be getting a similar call yourselves, and it won't be so bad if you have an idea what to expect. Somebody has got a bee in his bonnet about Mr. Cunningham's death.'

'Oh, what do you mean?' cried Abby. 'My husband died of a long and terrible illness.'

David pressed her shoulder. Distressed by her distress, he flicked a glance at the boy. Ladd showed no distress. He had that narrowed-in look upon his face. (David's soul

91

became prophetic.)

'I don't want to trouble you, Mrs. Crown,' the policeman was saying, 'but, as I say, it may be better if you know. This nut's idea is that somebody gave Mr. Cunningham . . . oh, probably sleeping pills or something of the sort . . . so that he died sooner than he should have.'

Under David's hand, Abby, although she did not seem to move, leaped, inside, as he could tell. And everything turned over for David. He felt stricken. What did Abby know? Had Hob . . . for God's sake, Hob! . . . put himself out, too soon? And did Abby know it? Oh, no, not possible. Yet, did she have reason to fear it? David felt afraid.

He said, stiff-lipped, 'You are talking about suicide?'

'Well, no,' said Douglas, 'the idea this nut had, seems more like murder.'

David could feel through his fingers and his arm the distress of the woman. He bent to her. 'Abby, just don't listen seriously. Just try to let it go over your head a minute.' He turned his head and said, 'Now, will you explain what you mean by murder?'

'What the voice on the telephone meant?' corrected Walter Douglas. 'I'm not so sure. Now, we have had instances of what you'd call a mercy killing and that is technically murder. Or, it's been known for some person to supply the sick one with the means to do away with

92

himself. But . . .'

Abby said, 'David?' He sat inside her fear, inside an aura. 'You don't believe that Hob took too many pills and died like that? Not Hob?' It must not be true. Abby would not have it so.

'No, no,' said David sharply. 'Don't you believe it. This was some crackpot. Mr . . . er . . . Douglas, is it? . . . *he* doesn't believe it.'

'What I was going to say,' said Douglas, 'I guess you probably don't realise, and this nut doesn't realise either, that it's pretty unlikely that a man can be poisoned or take poison in a hospital, or be murdered any other way, right under the doctors' noses and the doctors not suspect a thing at the time. So you are right when you say that I don't believe it. Of course . . .' He hesitated.

'Go on,' said David.

'Just the same, we are going to have to do a bit of checking. That's the policy. I'll talk to the doctors and all that. There was no autopsy?'

'No,' said David.

'I didn't permit it,' said Abby. 'I couldn't have borne it.' Her voice was high.

'Was one suggested, Mrs. Crown?'

'Somebody said for the advancement of science. But I didn't care about science. It could advance somewhere else. I cared about my husband.'

David said, 'Can we cut this short?' He was

93

concerned for her. He knew she had had a bad shock. He wished, now, that he had let her go out of the room, although she would have spent the time in lonely tension, imagining horrors.

The policeman was well aware of Abby's temperament, now. He said, 'Yes, but there is one thing more. And I'm looking for a little help from you. Now, as I say, I don't doubt that it is a crackpot. I don't know who. Maybe you can give me some idea who, if I tell you the rest of it.'

'Yes?' said David.

'This fellow said that Mr. Cunningham was murdered by *you*, Mr. Crown.'

'I see,' said David. Who saw. Clearly, now. He kept looking straight ahead at the policeman. On the left rim of his field of vision sat the boy, staring brilliantly.

But Abby now sagged. 'Well, then, of course it is just a crackpot,' she said with relief that was almost gay. 'Isn't that ridiculous?' She drew back from the gaiety. 'But isn't that terrible? Can't that be stopped?' Her eyes pleaded.

'If we can identify him, we can stop him,' the policeman said. He stood up, his pale eyes on David.

David thought, The crackpot is sitting right over there, watching with great interest and considerable glee. But how can I say so? He rose. He did not look to his left. He said smoothly, 'Thank you very much for letting us know about this, sir. At least, we'll be prepared.'

'You wouldn't be able to think of some person,' said Douglas, 'who has, say, a grudge against you, personally? And some kind of wild imagination?'

Don't describe him as plainly as that, thought David, or she will guess. He said, 'No. But I hope the matter is going to be taken seriously. I hope that you *will* check and do so thoroughly.'

'We expect to.' Something in the man's manner asked questions.

'Because if there is any more of this sort of thing,' said David, 'I would like proof of some kind to be turned up that will settle the truth of the matter.'

The policeman put his head to one side. 'The trouble with these birds, Mr. Crown, you can't reason with them,' he said warningly. 'It's not proof they are after. Well, I'll get along now. Maybe there won't be any more of it.' He glanced to his right, towards the boys. But David did not let his gaze drift even one degree to his left.

Ladd said, 'Stick around, Gare.'

Douglas said to Abby, 'Goodbye, ma'am. I'm sorry if it upset you.'

'It has,' said Abby forlornly. 'But thank you . . . I guess. And goodbye.

David went out into the hall and along it to the terrace door with the policeman. Now that they were alone and apart, the policeman said in his deep voice, 'The son, you think?'

'I think so. I couldn't prove it.'

'Not so easy to prove. *I* don't want to make a lot of trouble and misery for a lady like Mrs. Crown, any more than *you* do. But I'm going to tell you something. The Department doesn't appreciate being used.'

David said, 'I know that.'

'He's young. But to lay false information is an offence.'

'Yes, I know it is. Thank you.'

'Better get him straightened around,' the man said with an icy flash.

'I wish you'd tell me how to do it.'

The policeman shook his head. 'Well, sir, good luck is all I can say.'

They shook hands.

The two boys were at the library door. David turned to walk back towards them. He was angry. He walked fast. He never knew what he might, in that moment, have said or done, had the two of them not scampered up the stairs.

*   *   *

'Okay, you saw it!' Ladd was triumphant.

'Saw what?' Gary sank down upon Ladd's couch. 'Uncle Walt says it was a crackpot.' He glowered.

'But didn't you see dear David *crack*? He turned green! You must have seen it! The first time your uncle said what he said about "dying sooner." Right then! Old David, he knew what was up. And later on, when your uncle said "murder." Oh, wow! I'll bet he peed in his pants. Didn't you hear him try to put it off on suicide? Then when my mother asks, old David he says "No, no, no, not suicide." He was falling over his own feet. He didn't know where to look. Then he tries to fake it out. "Proof" he wants. Boy, that sounds great! Really great! You satisfied?'

'I don't get it,' said Gary sullenly. 'How could your dad get poisoned? Uncle Walt says they'd have found it out.'

'Maybe it wasn't poison. *He* thinks they'll never find out. Maybe they won't find out. But he's not so safe as he thinks he is. I'm absolutely sure, now.'

'You said you were sure before,' growled Gary. 'I don't see what's so great about figuring your dad was murdered. Sure gave your mom a bad time. I guess she must have been pretty crazy about your dad.'

'Until he was no good any more,' Ladd said with a bitter mouth. (He hadn't meant to say that. It wasn't smart to say that in front of Gary, who always looked dumb and chewed

97

like a cow if anybody said anything like that.)

'I think you should forget it,' said Gary bluntly. Ladd affected not to hear him.

'Listen, buddy,' said Gary. 'You might as well figure you're not going to get away with murder.'

'Because you'll talk, eh?' said Ladd nastily.

'Nope,' said Gary. 'Because you're not going to fool my Uncle Walt.'

Ladd made a gesture of pure impatience.

'Not much,' said Gary. Gary, the henchman, caught in a pair of opposing loyalties, chose one.

Ladd lifted his long lashes and looked at his former friend, buddy, and henchman coolly. 'Listen, what I mean . . . I *told* you. I want to get rid of him! I *told* you that. So I say I'll kill him. You know what I mean.'

'Get rid of him?'

'That's right. Get him out of my house,' said Ladd imperiously. 'Is there some law that says I have to have a murderer in the house?'

'Well, if that's what you mean . . .'

Ladd mused a while. 'How can you miss the point, Gare? He killed my father.' He spoke with sweet reason.

Gary moved his jaws. At last he said, 'That's what you keep on saying. Okay, if he did, they're going to find out. Uncle Walt is going to check. If there's evidence, he'll find it. *You* don't have to do anything.'

'Umm.' Ladd lay down on the floor in his

98

favourite position and turned his face away.

'Listen,' said Gary, 'Why don't you show Uncle Walt what your father wrote?'

'No.'

'Why not?'

'It's a message.'

'Yeah, but what message?'

'I can read it. I learned the alphabet long, long ago. Your uncle and dear David understand each other.'

'What do you mean by that?' Gary bristled.

'Oh, I don't know. You saw them shake hands.'

'What if they shook hands?'

'I don't know. I don't know.'

After a moment, Gary said, 'Want to go to the show?'

'No.'

'Want me to go home, see what I can find out while Uncle Walt is still there?'

'No,' said Ladd listlessly. In a moment, he said, 'Never did stop to think, did you, that a killer is dangerous?'

'Huh?'

'What if he gets rid of me?'

'Listen,' said Gary, *'he's* not going to . . . !'

'Well, if he does, you'll tell your uncle, I guess.' Ladd stretched.

Gary burst out, 'Why don't you take it a little bit easy.'

'Easy enough,' said Ladd lazily. 'No hurry, I guess.'

'That's right. Wait and see.'

'Yes, do that,' Ladd murmured.

'Hey, you know,' said Gary relaxing, 'it might not be such a bad deal to go into the Police Department.'

Ladd, face hidden, mumbled, 'Dangerous. But who wants to live forever, eh?'

'That's right and besides, they get a pretty good pension,' Gary said, 'if they stick it out.'

Ladd closed his eyes.

Nobody, nobody understood his position. He was alone. Wasn't he?

David was guilty. Guilt written on him. No doubt about it. But the trouble was that David Crown, heading up Cunningham Company, a prominent citizen, wasn't so easy to bring down. Gary was pretty naïve. As if there wouldn't be a conspiracy among those who were prominent, who had prestige. The doctors, for instance. They would conspire. They'd cover up. They wouldn't want a fuss raised. What, and undermine their lordly prestige? They were supposed to know what a man died of. They were never going to admit it if they didn't know, or if they'd covered up, or if they'd been wrong. And the law? The police? Yeah, Uncle Walt, dear Uncle Walt, he knew very well who was prominent and who wasn't and how the pattern mustn't be upset. He and David Crown understood each other, all right. Cover-cover-cover-cover. Hob Cunningham was dead and buried. What if he had died a little soon? He had *been* dying,

100

hadn't he? So that was okay with everyone. Except his son. Except his son.

Knowledge was relief, was burden, was lonely, was not lonely enough. Old David knew. Knew that Ladd knew. Sure, old David even knew who had done the telephoning. That rigid neck. He'd never looked. Didn't dare. Ladd, who had waited for the look that never came, knew this *because* it never came. Which was too subtle for such as Gary Fenwick. Dumb Gary, who thought his Uncle Walt was going to check. Oh, laugh . . .

Only the two of them knew . . . Ladd rolled over.

All right. *Alone.* Kill the wicked. Plan it. Plot it. Let nothing else matter. Nothing. Plan, not what to do, but how. Alone.

CHAPTER SEVEN

'I'm all right now.' Abby reached for his hand. 'But it scared me so.'

'What scared you?'

'Just for a minute, that's all. I . . . had it all so clear. He was a dear man and I loved him dearly, as you know, David, and then he got this horrible thing, and he died. Oh, don't you see? For a minute . . . to have to revise the whole thing . . .' Then Abby said, shockingly, 'But if he did, David, I couldn't condemn him.

101

I can't bear pain.'

'Please . . .'

'But of course, Hob didn't.' She sat up straighter. 'And I hope they catch that insane person and put him away. To say such things.'

David couldn't follow the twisting moods. 'Yes, darling, but what scared you?'

'You see, when Hob first went back . . .'

'To the hospital?'

'Yes. Well, I had some pills for pain that my doctor had given me. And Hob had taken one, once. I think when he had a tooth extracted. So he said to me that my pills were .. a . . . hell of a lot more powerful than anything they had around that place. And he wished he had some of them. So of course, I brought him all I had.'

'You'—David swallowed—'brought him some pills?'

'Yes, I did. Of course, I did. He said he wished he had them.' Her eyes were hurt.

'I understand, darling, but what were they?'

'I don't know. I don't ask. I just take what the doctor tells me to take. I just knew they were for pain.'

David's breath moved inward with slow care. 'Did you see Hob take any, in the hospital?'

'No, I didn't.' She used her handkerchief.

'But he kept them?'

'Oh, yes. He thanked me and he kept them.' Her tears started.

'Were they in a bottle?'

'One of those little plastic cylinders.'

'Many pills?'

'Oh yes, all I had. Almost full.'

'Your prescription?'

'Yes. David, why . . . ?'

'Abby, were they dangerous?'

'I don't know. But it said on the label how many to take and how often.'

(Lord, she doesn't see her own inconsistency. Lord, help me think) 'How could Hob keep a prescription of yours in a hospital room?'

'I don't know. I think he put them in the little drawer with his toothpaste.'

'They must have been found. When was this, Abby?'

Her long throat worked. 'Oh, a long time . . .'

'A long time before he died? How long?'

'Oh, weeks. You're worse than the police,' said Abby. 'Why are you asking?'

'I'd better find out what they were.'

'But he *couldn't* have. The man *said* so. He said the doctors would have known.' She would begin to tremble in a moment.

'I'm sure that's right. I'm sure they would,' he soothed.

'Then what does it matter what they were?'

'It doesn't,' said David, relaxing. 'There is no connection.' He believed, himself, that the doctors would have known, had Hob taken strange (and lethal) medication. David tried to feel relieved. And yet—it was true that Hob had died rather mercifully. David had always

103

felt, although perhaps never clearly stated it even to himself, that Hob, having made his will, had then in a businesslike way simply gone ahead and died. It would have been like him.

Abby had clasped her hands. She said, 'It tears me to pieces, even to think about it. Oh, David, if he did, if he had to . . . because there was such wicked pain . . . Oh, David . . .' She was going to fall over. 'I think if he had told me why he wanted my pills, I'd still have brought them.'

'Don't begin to believe it, now,' David warned sharply. 'Don't do that, Abby.' He knew the first step to belief was to be able to imagine. He rose from where he had been crouching and his knee cracked. 'In the first place, Hob was probably only kidding, to say he wanted them. He took your gift. He wouldn't hurt your feelings. But he would never put you on such a spot, either. We can certainly believe that much. Your pills were confiscated the next day, by some nurse, no doubt. Strange medicine just does not lie around in a hospital. So there is no point in thinking any more about it. And do not believe two things at once, darling.'

'I'm so foolish,' she said and used her handkerchief. 'But then, I always have been. You love me, anyway.'

Abby's mixture. A little childish, yet able to be amused at her own childishness. And able

104

to tell a simple truth. He did love her, anyway. He looked down upon her lovely silver hair, her head, that darling mystery. She seemed to have dismissed the point that someone had accused David of murder. Why? Because she thought it so absurd?

David was not one to dismiss absurdity, just as such. He knew that he would check—oh very gingerly—and find out just what Abby's pills might do and whether Hob had shown any symptoms that might pertain. He did not believe that Hob was a suicide. But it was wise to protect himself, and Abby, by some evidence.

Abby got out of the chair. 'What a mess I must look,' she cried. 'Oh, I'm so glad . . .'

He stared at her, unable to follow.

'. . . that none of it seemed to upset Ladd the least bit. Did it?' she said radiantly.

'Didn't . . . seem to,' he said, marvelling.

'I thought he took it all so well. So much better than I.' (David felt his very soul pinched.) 'Like a man,' said Abby mistily. And then, with one of her sudden changes, 'David, take me out to dinner? Somewhere charming? I feel,' said Abby, 'like being taken out to dinner.'

'All right.'

'Oh.' It was as if he had surprised her with an invitation. 'Then I must do something about this face. Maybe I'll lie down a little bit, with goo on it. Then dress.'

'Good programme.'

'Ah, David, you are so dear and so good to me.' Abby kissed him. She went upstairs.

*   *   *

David marvelled.

Abby knew that to go out to dinner meant the two of them. She knew that Ladd would not go along. Did that mean that she knew? He left it for a mystery.

He contemplated the spot that he was on. He had not told Abby, bluntly, directly (or honestly) that he believed her son to have been the crackpot on the telephone. He had not forced her to contemplate what the boy had done. Although David knew very well that he might be forced to do this, and perhaps very soon, he did not wish to do it now. He did not wish to 'tear her to pieces'. He would rather not. He could not see that it would help anyone, in any way . . . not yet.

What was he going to do, then?

Think, he advised himself. You are supposed to have a brain.

Let us be orderly. (Alternative Number One.) If the boy really believed that David had, in some way, done away with Hob, arranged for him to die sooner than was natural, why, that explained a great deal! That, then, was the basis for the hostility, for the wall, for everything. But, since it made all the rest reasonable, such an erroneous belief could be attacked with reason. With the kind of proof the police, the court, or reasoning minds accept.

There would have been, too, a reason for the boy to have acquired such a belief. Some misinterpretation. Something to be found out, attacked, and by reason shown to be an error. Oh yes, all this would follow, if the boy did truly believe.

But (Alternative Number Two) what if the phone call was just malice? That would mean something more difficult, perhaps impossible, to attack. Some callous, criminal meanness. An abnormal, or at least a very ugly and undesirable, state. An illness.

Which was the case with the boy? How to discover? David considered talking to him, now. Considered having to send a twenty-year-old playmate home in order to achieve privacy. Considered Abby, if he were to do this.

Abby first, of course.

He had asked her, once, how Hob had dealt with what she called Ladd's moods.

'Oh, I could usually coax him out of them before Hob came home. But I must say that if there was any least trace left, Hob always knew it. And he'd . . . well, he'd just go right against it. He'd just *have at it.* I can't explain.'

'But it worked?' David had asked.

'I couldn't bear those times. Quarrelling upsets me, David. I can't help that. I don't see why people can't just be courteous to each other.'

'Do you mean that they quarrelled?'

'It wouldn't go as far as that.'

'I don't get the picture, Abby.'

'Well—Hob, you know, used to ride right over moods. Although not,' she had added thoughtfully, 'not mine.' Abby's mixture.

Now David began to wonder. Had she spoiled that boy rotten, forever 'coaxing' him? Yet Abby could be, in her own way, very firm. She had sent him away from the table, last evening, for being a naughty child. Done it in a sweet and gentle voice, but done it. If her standard was politeness, she at least insisted upon her standard. Abby's courtesy was . . . adamant. David smiled to himself, and left that.

He considered Hob. When Hob 'rode over' a mood, as he would have done in a noisy and cheerful fashion, did the boy think him insensitive and too severe? A strong man, who indulged Abby because she had enchanted him, had Hob, in truth, been too severe with, for instance, a trait of Abby's turning up in his male child?

David left all these thoughts. He did not like himself for having them. And besides, who knew? Who could ever say? *However* this boy had got off on the course he was now following, he had to be straightened around. And quickly.

Confront him? That was David's natural impulse. Have at him, then? Now? Say to him, 'Look here, I know and the police know who made that phone call and you can be in very bad trouble if you do not straighten around. Now first, your father was not murdered at all, and second, I have never murdered anyone. What is it going to take to get the idea out of your head? You tell me what it takes and I'll provide it.'

But would that work?

Or say, 'Look here, you are going to distress your mother beyond what she can bear.' Would that reach him? David winced.

He sat in Hob Cunningham's house and could not feel sure enough to act. He was a reasonable man, and more. What was it that Aaron had said of him? Kind, honest, patient, and understanding. All the most respected virtues of our modern age. But the virtues were incompatible here. David could not clearly see how to be both kind and honest in this instance.

Still, he could be reasonable. He would not, for instance, act in anger or in haste. Or in any more ignorance than he could humanly help. No, not until he knew as much as it was possible for him to know.

But was it possible to find out what the boy was thinking, when he could not communicate with the boy? He thought, ruefully, of his own good cheer only this morning. Now he believed that, although he could certainly march upstairs and ask the question, 'Do you believe that I killed your father?' he would precipitate some kind of open conflict and distress in the house, but he would not necessarily, or even probably, get the true answer.

An oblique approach occurred to him. Could he find out through Gary Fenwick? That loyal henchman was obviously in on the telephone plot, for it had been known where Walter Douglas was on a Sunday. Maybe, maybe, thought David. I'm wilier than he is, at least. Devious, treacherous, to go round about. No matter, thought David grimly. If it is the only feasible way to go. After all, the boy did not confront *me*, but went round about.

He began to muse on Aaron's words. The cream of western civilisation? Or a super-hypocrite? Which am I? Neither. Neither. A man, loving, worrying, willing, wanting, like any man alive since the dawn, civilised or not. But a man who watches his own motivations because he knows what the devil can do and does not care to be possessed.

Yet. Both. Both. A man who examines all he can find in himself and knows very well that there is much he has not found yet. But who would now pretend. He would in cold blood hide the hot truth, that what he would most like to do, in pure and primitive rage, would be to go up there, now, and hit, strike, beat that

110

boy, give him physical pain for punishment. In a fury of judgment. Or revenge?

Not for me, he thought ruefully. For one thing, were I to beat up the boy, then he would be one-up on me, among my peers, within our system. He heard the vibration of their descent. Four feet on the stairs. He let them go.

David Crown sat still in Hob Cunningham's house. An intruder? Meaning well, but an intruder just the same?

But, God help him, an honest man. Why had he not said openly to the policeman when he had been asked, 'Yes, I think I know your telephoner. There he is.' Why had he not? To spare Abby, of course. Even the policeman, who already must have suspected, had wanted to spare Abby.

And now Abby 'felt like' being taken out to dinner. And would be.

He perceived that Abby had her power. That there could be a tyranny of weakness.

So David had let the boy go, had not confronted him, lost the chance, for this day, this evening. Sat here, being reasonable. The trouble was, being also honest, he knew how the heart could bend the reason and was bending and using his own. He wondered whether Abby, having Hob's heart, had ever bent Hob's reason. Of course she had. Of course she had. Not Abby, but Abby's needs.

What about the boy, then? How could a

grown man expect the boy to keep reason clear and bright and straight, when the man could, even now, see his own bending, bending, for a darling woman's sake?

No, he could not expect too much from the boy. David saw deeper. If the boy 'believed' that David was a killer, maybe . . . no, almost certainly . . . it was not his 'reason' that believed. And in the case (which was close enough to Alternative Number Two), what was there to do?

Be kind and patient and try to understand.

But do nothing?

CHAPTER EIGHT

About a quarter to ten, on Monday morning, Rafe Lorimer slapped sandals upon stone steps. 'There you are, Abby.'

'Good morning,' she said cheerily. She was cutting faded blossoms away from her roses. 'Where were you all day yesterday?'

'I,' said Rafe, 'was writing a poem.' He was wearing his usual costume; his hair was rumpled on his head. 'Abby dear, lend me your ears?'

'Of course.'

'Where is everyone?'

'David's at the plant, naturally. Ladd is upstairs, I think. Cleona is in the kitchen. Here am I.'

'Could we go indoors, please?'

Abby pouted, regretting the open day.

'Felicia has gone to the corner. I would rather she didn't . . . uh . . . know.'

'It is about Felicia?'

'Yes, please.'

Abby sighed and dumped her handful of blooms, stripped off her garden gloves.

They went into the library, which was sunny at this hour. Rafe said, 'Abby dear, I won't take long. I can't. I have an appointment. A committee of ladies. It seems I am inveigled into addressing a group of young people at the Wednesday Club. They are beginning an art class. Did you know?'

'No,' said Abby, who was not a clubwoman. 'How nice, Rafe. Would you like some coffee?'

'No, no. Thank you. I have only a minute. I'm snatching it.' He did his accordion smile. 'Because of your son and my daughter and what's happened.

'My . . . *Ladd* and Felicia?' Abby blinked.

'Now, Abby, neither you nor I would be so very much pleased by any romance between them. Shall we just face that?'

She bit her lips and furrowed her brow.

'There will be none,' said Rafc. 'That's what I came to tell you.'

Abby put her head to one side. 'Why, thank you,' she said gently. 'Now surely you have time for one cup?'

'I must speak to the boy. I wanted to tell you first.'

'But tell me what?'

'Ladd waited for her, evidently.'

'What do mean? When?'

'On Saturday evening.'

'Oh?'

'Oh yes, that is why she never did come back. Now, there was some kind of quarrel between them. Felicia is heart-sick about it.'

'Why, I *am* sorry.' Now she was troubled.

'Because,' said Rafe with the faintest touch of triumph, 'she happens to be a tender-hearted girl and she did not enjoy having to refuse his advances.'

'Oh Rafe,' said Abby mournfully, and only just, without laughter, 'you must be confused.'

Rafe said, 'No, I think not. You don't often go out to the pool, do you? Whereas I, from my studio, can very often see and sometimes hear. You may not have observed them together, as I have done.'

'Ladd and *Felicia*?'

'Oh yes. Certainly. He had been keeping very close to home and the pool. Abby, dear, you must have noticed that much. The boy is devoted to you, as you know. He is quite aware of the fact that you and Felicia never did hit it off. So—can't you see his conflict?'

Abby continued to look puzzled.

'Now, she is unhappy and, I daresay, he is unhappy. Oh, it will pass, as all things must.

But you and I can, perhaps, help our young people?'

'Felicia told you that he . . . *What* did you say?' Abby leaned forward.

'We trust each other,' said Rafe in his fatuous way. 'Yes, she told me. I want to make sure that the boy knows this is final. Can you help him, Abby?'

Abby, her face a little pink, said, innocently and wistfully, 'What am I to do, Rafe?'

'Why, point out that they are cousins. Or . . . that it isn't suitable, for many reasons. Or . . . that there are other fish in the sea. You'll know what you must say.'

'I must say, right now,' said Abby, 'that I *don't*, at all. To me, this is very, very strange.'

'Oh my,' said Rafe. 'Not at all. At the dinner table? His outburst?'

'He is sorry for that,' she said softly. 'Forgive him?'

'But didn't it come immediately after Felicia spoke to him?'

'Did she speak to him?'

'Oh yes.'

'What did she say?'

'I don't remember,' said Rafe. 'But it must have hurt him somehow. And he lashed out, of course. Easily forgiven, if only we understand. Isn't that so?'

Abby sighed deeply. 'You understand it? You think it was on Felicia's account?'

'I do.'

'Well, I'll ask him about this . . . did you say a quarrel?'

'Please do, Abby. I'll want to talk to him, too.'

'Please don't, Rafe. Let me.'

'Well . . .'

'I still think there is something . . . confused. Are you sure?'

Rafe said, 'I am sure of one thing. I am afraid that I'll have to insist that Felicia not be harassed or importuned.'

'*Advances*,' said Abby suddenly. 'That's what you said. Now you say "harass" and "importune."' Her voice became gentle, with the faintest touch of a humorous dryness. 'I can't believe Ladd meant to do anything of the sort to Felicia—really. But of course I thank you for coming.'

Rafe's face was pinker and his chin was drawn in. 'I came in all good faith. I do not want a quarrel between our houses.'

'Oh, Rafe dear,' cried Abby, 'there won't be. Will you take some coffee?'

'No, thank you, I . . .'

'Would you like *me* to speak to Felicia?'

'I think . . . better not,' said Rafe, rather gloomily.

His ardent good intentions had run into her very polite but total scepticism. He took himself into the stair-hall. Ladd Cunningham was on the stairs.

'Oh, does she?' The voice was light; the

116

fingertips slid and caressed the glowing wood; the boy looked down, with his head held high. He was 'looking down his nose.'

The back of Rafe's neck ached. He felt old and foolish and furious.

But Abby spoke behind him and said, 'Yes, please, dear, I would like a minute. You must go, Rafe? I think you said there was a committee of ladies?'

'Yes, I have an appointment.' Rafe stalked towards the terrace door. He looked back over his shoulder and called, 'But *I* want a word with you, later on.'

Nobody answered him. Ladd came down the six steps with a swift tattoo of his young feet. His mother had drawn back into the library and he went through that door. Rafe, left standing in the stair-hall, began to affirm his right to *be,* and to be heard, by an angry and stubborn stillness of his feet.

*   *   *

'Better close the door,' Abigail said, smiling.

Ladd closed the door.

'There is no point in troubling Cleona with our problems, do you think?' She sat down, in her graceful way. The boy stood against the closed door.

'Dear, it seems that you have upset Felicia Lorimer. Somehow.' Abby's air was the opposite of severe. She was ready to discuss an

117

amusing misunderstanding.

But Ladd said, 'I'm sorry,' with no expression and almost without moving his lips.

Abby seemed surprised. 'I'm afraid I hadn't realised that you were very much interested.'

'In what?' Ladd said. (All this was extraneous. Of no matter. Lonely, he stood, with the burden on him, and his mother babbled of green girls.)

'Felicia is a sweet little thing; of course. Do you find her . . . attractive?'

'Why?' he said.

'Darling,' said Abby with frustration, 'that's not any kind of question. I don't understand it. Come over and sit down, please. And tell me, did you meet Felicia, Saturday evening?'

The boy did not move from his position. 'What about it?' he said impatiently.

Abby said, touching her throat, 'Oh, dear, then Rafe is right?'

'Right about what?' (He wanted to go. Be alone, think, plot, plan. Didn't she realise that he had to kill someone?)

'That you and she have become better friends than I had . . . realised. And now there has been this quarrel. He says,' said Abby with elaborate calm, 'that Felicia is not as fond of you as you would like her to be?' She looked up, smiling question.

The boy thought: Lies! Lies! And no *time* for them.

His mother said, 'Then you do find Felicia

118

Lorimer attractive?'

'Then you do find,' mimicked the boy, 'David Crown attractive?' (He hadn't meant to say that.)

'What?' Abby sucked in her breath and said, 'We are speaking about something that happened on Saturday night. Did you quarrel with Felicia, dear?'

(Quarrel? he thought. And that's not polite. But neither is murder.) His face fell to bitter stone.

His mother said gently. 'I only want to understand. Please?' Then, softly, 'Ladd, I've asked you a question.'

'Mother, I've asked you a question,' he mimicked, melodiously. His head bent to the right, his eyes were cold.

She sat very straight. Her eyes filled up with the old familiar reproachful suffering. 'Rafe tells me that you made "advances".' Abby's pretty mouth showed fastidious distaste. 'I can't *believe* that. Felicia, evidently—'

'Evidently. Evidentially. Evi*dence*.' (He was thinking, Liars! Liars! Let me alone! It's not important!)

'Oh, Ladd, what is the matter?' Abby rose and came towards him, ready for tears and caresses.

'Don't touch me,' he said, with an underlying scream.

'Darling . . .'

(Oh, she was so innocent. She was so

bewildered. She was so hurt. She was going to cry and that would help a lot. He had no *time* for it.) 'Oh, God, you make me sick,' he said to her with loathing.

Her face crumpled. She put out one hand.

'Don't talk to *me*,' he said frantically. 'Don't talk to *me*. *I* don't go to bed with the first willing one that comes along.'

Abby had turned white. 'Ladd, aren't you well?' She begged him to be ill.

'Well. Well. Very well, Mother.'

She stepped backwards, looking frightened. She pulled herself up and said, 'I don't know what's happened between you and this girl—'

'—You and this man.'

'Don't say that. I don't understand you. Just tell me—What is the matter? You know—surely you know I only want to help you.'

'Then, help.' He took a step. 'Mother get rid of him.'

'What?'

'Kick him out. Throw him out. Tell him to get out.'

'I think,' she wailed, 'you must be crazy!'

There was a sharp rap at the door. Ladd turned around and yanked it open. Rafe Lorimer stood there. He said, 'Abby, do you need me?' His face wore its pleated smile.

The boy's face turned demonic. 'You, too?' he said. Then, with a mocking bow, 'Be my guest. Be my mother's guest. Certainly she needs you. My father is dead. And you know it too, don't you?'

'You must not speak to me like that, young man. Nor to your mother.' It was Rafe's fate to look ridiculous in anger.

'I'll say what I want.'

'I will not listen.'

'You listen to your lying daughter. Lying daughter! Oh good! Very good! I wouldn't lie; that was her trouble.' Ladd's voice was cracking with hysterical laughter.

'You had better leave this room,' said Rafe sternly. 'You are upsetting your mother.'

The boy said, laughing, 'Words. Words. Don't you ever listen to the meaning of words? You old fool! Sneak!'

'Sticks and stones,' said Rafe, pink and puffed up and ridiculous.

Ladd said, 'Get out of my way. Don't bother me.' He lifted his right arm. Rafe wilted out of his path. The boy rushed away.

*   *   *

Rafe heard the racking sobs and saw Abby's body convulsing in the chair. He was frightened. 'Abby, don't, Abby. He must be out of his mind. Really. Don't pay attention. He didn't know what he was saying. He couldn't have known.'

But she sobbed.

'Please, try to be a little . . . a little . . . calmer.' Rafe didn't know what to do. 'Shall I call the doctor, Abby?'

'No. Yes.' She writhed. 'Call David. I need him. He loves me.'

'I don't know his number,' said Rafe frantically. 'Everybody loves you.' Rafe, catapulted out of the world he had invented, didn't know where he was.

CHAPTER NINE

Ladd Cunningham ran through the garden, down to the drive, back to his car. He began to hear female voices coming from Rafe's studio, just the other side of the hedge. The women's voices gushed, babbled, hooted and twittered. Ladd's hands opened and closed, opened and closed. Women!

He wrenched his thought to Rafe, the meddling old idiot. And his lying daughter. He would like to tell *her* . . . He stepped to peer through the gap in the hedge. All he could see was a strange car, standing in the Lorimers' driveway with a man in it. Intolerable! Intolerable! In his deep trouble, to have been persecuted by gnats! A liar, and an old fool who was her dupe, and meddlers, both of them. How dared . . .! How dared . . .! How dared . . .! His rage began to turn to ice and his whole soul gathered to a knife-edge. Ladd sidled through the gap. He did not know what he might not do. He felt such power. He could punish. He could publish what they were.

He reined himself in . . . narrowed in. As he drew near the car he said, 'Hi.' And then, shyly, 'Oh, excuse me. I thought I knew you, sir.'

'Harper is my name. I'm just my wife's chauffeur this morning.' The man was old, all grey skin, sharp bones, and fierce hair. He was old, but spry, and he was bored by this waiting.

Ladd turned his head and looked towards the studio. 'What's going on in there?'

'Bunch of women,' the man answered, pleased to be using his voice. 'Came to ask this artist fellow to make a speech.'

Ladd's ear caught the flavour of scorn on the word 'artist'.

'Who?' he asked.

'This Rafael Lorimer. Uh . . . you the Lorimer boy?'

'No, I just live around here.' Ladd was pretending to be vaguely troubled. His wits whirled, so sharp, so shining. His eyelids were white on the tan face.

'They want to kick off this new art course,' Mr. Harper said, 'for teenagers.'

'Teenagers?' said Ladd, artfully breathless. White lids flew up. He knew what he was going to say. He had remembered the inside of Rafe's studio the last time he had seen it. This was good. This was better. This was perfect. Just a question of how to say it. Ah, but he had

123

advised Gary. All you had to do was say it *'as if.'*

'Say, where is he, do you know?' The old man squirmed.

'Oh, I guess he's around,' said Ladd. 'Say, Mr. Harper . . . ?'

'Yep.'

'You're an older man.'

'I guess that's right, all right.'

'Well, see, I don't know what I should do.' Ladd hung his head.

'About what?'

'About . . . something. I wish I could ask you.'

'Why don't you ask your dad,' said Mr. Harper warily, sensing he knew not what.

'I can't. My dad is dead.'

'Sorry, son. I guess that's pretty tough.'

'It's not about me.'

'No? What about, then?'

'About this . . . artist.'

'What about him?'

'Well, I happen . . . Listen, I didn't *want* to see anything. I couldn't help it.' (Oh, he would feel like puking, *'if'.*)

Mr. Harper shifted in the seat, his interest kindled. 'What's this?'

'I've been keeping still, because . . . Well, it's just impossible, that's all. Only . . . you say he is supposed to make a speech to some teenagers?'

'That's the idea, I guess.'

124

'Well, I can tell you, he's a great one!' said Ladd viciously. (His duty 'if'. Yes, it would be his reluctant duty.)

'Why?' the man snapped. Ladd twitched and stepped backward. 'Come on. Why?'

'Well, maybe you know he has a . . . I can't do this.'

'Yes, you can. You can talk to me,' coaxed the old man, perishing of curiosity.

'I . . . got to tell somebody. But how can I tell my mom a thing like this? I mean, I couldn't.'

'As you say, I'm a man and older. Don't be afraid.'

'No, sir.' Ladd came closer. The old man seemed to have excellent hearing. So Ladd spoke low. 'He has this daughter. She's probably about seventeen now.' He looked at his hand. His fingers were on the warm metal of the car. Power was in their very tips, the power of his mind. *(As if. As if. As if.)*

'I got the impression he has two kids,' the old man said. 'Right?'

'Yes, but the son . . . the son goes away to college.'

'Does?'

'Well, see, when he goes away, then that leaves just this artist and the girl, living all alone here.' Ladd took his hand away and stepped back. His face was sad stone.

Old Mr. Harper put his head out the window and looked up at the shabby old

125

house.

'I didn't . . . believe me . . . I didn't want to see anything and I wish I never had.' Ladd looked as if he would fly away.

The old man's hair seemed to bristle. 'What was it that you saw?'

'It's kinda awful . . . kinda sickening . . .' They stared, eye to eye. Ladd's eyes had a bright horror. (Because it would be horrible, 'if.')

'Now, wait a minute. You say you *saw*?' The old man croaked.

'Well, it just happens that I can look right into his . . .'

'Yes.'

'Bedroom.'

'Oh, lord,' said Mr. Harper.

'She . . . Look, I don't want to get them into trouble. I mean not the girl. She doesn't . . . I mean, he is her father, so wouldn't she have to do what he says?'

'Oh, lord.' The old man had the door open and was getting out of the car now, putting one shaky leg to the ground.

'And her mother's been dead a long time. So there's nobody . . .' I know it's not my business . . .'

'Oh, lord.' Mr. Harper hung on to the car door. 'If this is true . . .' His eyes were sharp under the bushy brows.

'Listen . . . Please . . .' Ladd cried. 'Maybe it isn't. I wish it wasn't. I've been practically sick.'

He staggered. 'I didn't know what I ought to do. I never looked again. I couldn't. Listen, I don't want to get mixed up in anything like this. Only I got to get it off my mind.'

'I understand. I understand,' said the old man harshly.

Ladd put both hands over his face. 'See, he is an artist. He doesn't go to work or anything. I said to myself maybe he doesn't think it's so . . . bad. Maybe it isn't—I mean, for some kinds of people. Only . . . she's not very popular, you know. She doesn't go round with kids her own age. She . . . hasn't got anybody . . .'

'Oh, lord,' the old man said and turned his back and began to walk towards the studio.

Ladd peered through his fingers. The old man went into the remodelled stable. The sound of female voices died, abruptly. And so much for the lying daughter and the meddling old fool, too. Words, that's all it took! Ladd moved. Fluidly, he slipped through the hedge and into his car. His ears felt a foot long, waiting for something. An explosion?

But what he could hear was the slap of Rafe's sandals. The boy slid far down in his seat and did not breathe. The sandals came, slap, slap, on the concrete. Slap, slap, they passed. The hedged rustled. Rafe was a little late to his appointment, the old fool! Teach him to trust a liar! Teach a father to trust his treacherous no-good child!

127

Foot and hand, ready to go, Ladd froze, suffering in an instant a flash of clear light. *I am sick.* (Yes, he knew it.) For upon him had fallen the weight of the memory of all the years of Rafe, like an old pussycat around the place. Rafe and his chatter, his smile, his earnest puttering, his . . . harmlessness.

But it was too late now. Nobody could help it now. He, was sick, in himself, enough to die. Would *rather.* But he hardened. There was dear David still. And nothing else really mattered. So a gun was what he had to have. Too late for anything else. So hurry, hurry. Not much more time, Father.

Oh God, he thought, if I had his keys, I'd take his car and smash it and smash it so no one else could ever touch what has belonged to him.

He put his own car into gear and roared backward out of the drive.

*   *   *

Felicia was walking home from the corner grocery store, carrying a big brown paper bag. She thought to herself that life goes on, as they say, but somehow or other it goes on most obviously on a Monday morning. Ah well, then, if it went on there had to be meals and if meals, then expeditions for supplies—so here she was on the sidewalk just as if she hadn't had her heart broken.

She was wearing a tight pair of black bermudas and a tailored green-and-white checked blouse that covered the mark on her shoulder. Her dark hair was caught up in a rubber band and hung in a long tail from the crown of her head. One thong threaded through her bare toes to hold each sandal's sole to the sole of her foot. She might have been twelve years old.

But, as she ambled through patches of sun and shade along the pleasant suburban street where she had lived all her life, it seemed to her to have been a long life.

Her childhood seemed to her to have been long and sunny with delights, in the days when she had had a father and a mother and a brother and, in succession, two dogs whose whole lifetimes she could remember. But ever since twelve—yes, since about then—the sun had played in and out of cloud. She had found out that her family did not live just like all other families—whether for better or for worse. That her house had neither the physical nor the mental furniture that the houses of her playmates had. And a little later she had found out that she was not going to be a pretty girl nor was she going to be able to pretend to be pretty by wearing the teen-fad clothes that most girls wore. Especially party dresses. She was not going to very many parties. She hadn't the mental furniture that made her an easy guest.

Felicia had been quietly reckoning up these differences when—all suddenly in a day—her mother had died. And she, desperate to help her stricken father, had tried never to grieve where he could see or hear her grief. Today she was remembering that time, that very bad time. When people said such stupid things. Cousin Abby had said *all* the stupid things, every one. Felicia had curled up like a snail in its shell to protect herself.

Only one person . . . as she was remembering today . . . had said a thing that had meant a great deal to her. It wasn't the minister, either. (Felicia Lorimer belonged to a church and faithfully attended. It was another little difference, but all her own.) No, it was not the minister. It was Mr. Cunningham. Mr. Hob Cunningham, who had come upon her on one of those very bad afternoons the week after the funeral, when she was trying to reach a peach on the tree and he had reached up and picked it for her—not just any peach, but the very one she'd had her eye on. He didn't say, 'I'm so sorry,' or, 'Your mother was a lovely person.' Or, 'You must not be unhappy, little girl. She wouldn't have wanted that.'

He had said, 'Shakes you up, all right, doesn't it, Felicia? Yep, it's the one thing you hit and hit hard. And he'll shake the nonsense out of you, Old Brother Death, when he comes.'

She could remember looking up at him and thinking, Oh, strong and true! And feeling a lot of nonsense draining out of her, leaving a hard peace.

Now she thought, I wonder if I liked Ladd Cunningham, in part, for his father's sake. Because he was so strong and true. I guess poor Ladd is—neither.

And she thought, Old Brother Death came for Mr. Cunningham so that he didn't get to see his son the way he is. That would have been hard for him. No, not for him. Or at least, not too hard, because he was strong and true.

She dreamed no dreams of a sentimental vindication, about Ladd Cunningham. She did not fantasy a day when he would come to her, contrite, knowing the hurt he had given her innocence, anxious to atone for it. Such a dream was nonsense. Why, if he had any idea that he had hurt her so, he'd hate her! He didn't hate *her,* now. He didn't even know her. He hated something about her that was only a mistake of his own. A hateful something.

But it might not have been. Felicia was not so silly as to think that sex was evil. No, if there had been between them the sweet magnetism of the flesh, it might have been lovely. And there might have been such a time. But she had been so far from such thoughts—in that moment, Saturday. It was strange to her that his intuition had been so faulty. In fact, the whole incident scarcely had anything to do with Felicia. Well, she didn't know him then. And now she never would.

You might as well hit a hard thing hard. So the aching Sunday was over, and Ladd Cunningham was over and out.

So . . . school next week and her senior year. Next year (Justin said) she could get away. She scuffled along. She saw a tassel fallen from a tree—such casual beauty. Beauty so lavishly falling all around that you didn't even notice. Well, then, in spite of a wide world she had never seen (and in spite of Justin), here, where she walked, was the world? Was it not?

So musing, her feet took her in at the familiar turn, to travel down the drive towards the kitchen door. A strange car was there, two women in it, and two more standing beside it.

Felicia came on her bare brown legs, with her unpainted face childish over the big brown bag, looking about twelve years old. She was thinking, Why should anything bigger happen to you in some *other* place? A freakish and alliterative sentence popped into her mind. 'Can your heart be broken better in Bombay?'

The women had stopped talking at sight of her. She stopped walking and said, smiling more at her own whimsy than at them, 'Hallo. I'm Felicia Lorimer. Are you looking for my father?'

'No, no,' said one of them tensely. 'We're waiting for Mr. Harper.'

132

'I see.' Felicia nodded and went up the steps and into the kitchen. She didn't 'see.' She hadn't the faintest idea who Mr. Harper was or where or why they were waiting at the spot. She was thinking her own thoughts. Can you worry worse in Winnipeg? Or dig death deeper in Detroit? (Old Brother Death) No, no, she thought proudly, it is just as hard, right here. Just as hard—every bit. This is the world and I am alive in it. The ache and the pain seemed to be loosening and letting her go. Her body felt lighter. She moved around the kitchen, putting the food away.

*   *   *

Under the kitchen window the women were talking fiercely. They were all concerned with duty. One of them kept saying, in a fluster, 'Better wait for Mr. Harper. Just wait for Mr. Harper.' It was their duty, she insisted, because it was only fair to wait for Mr. Harper. One was militant. The girl must be taken away. Surely some agency in the community had the power to take her away. Why, it was the duty of a decent community not to permit such things to be! For her own sake, for everyone's sake, she must, must, must be taken away. Another wanted to go home at once and threatened to walk there. She had a daughter in high school who knew the girl. No, she would not take the girl into her home. She had

133

her duty to her own. It was too bad. It was just too bad. *But.* She knew what her duty was. The fourth lady thought it was her duty to keep her mouth shut; she kept saying so.

Little Felicia, in the kitchen, was not, in spite of her philosophy and contrary to her newly present resolution, listening, at all, to what was going on in the world that she was in. The first sound that attracted her attention was a long '*ssssssh*'. Then, her mind played back the loud sentence that had been shushed. 'And he ought to be whipped, disgusting old beast.'

Felicia stood still She heard a man speak. 'Let's get out of here, ladies.'

'But what?'

'What did he say?'

A car door banged. 'He says he knows the boy and the boy is crazy.'

'*Tch, tch!*' 'Well, he would . . .' 'He'd have to . . .'

'Come on. Hurry up, please,' the man said, 'I want to get going!'

'But is it true, Mr. Harper? That's the point, after all.'

'Whether it's true or not,' said Mr. Harper, 'this is a terrible business, I'll tell you that.' Car door banged.

'Law?'

Car engine into noise.

'I say, a law?' A female speaking.

Motor racing. Then foot off the throttle and

134

lever into gear.

'Oh, pity the little girl!'

Then, shrill, 'Mr. Harper, I want to go home, right now, if you don't mind.'

Car noise receding.

*　　　*　　　*

Felicia drifted across the kitchen and looked out at the quiet yard where she knew every tree, every stone. The old stable beside the camphor tree was quiet.

She pushed the screen door. She let it back behind her gently, not wanting it to slap shut with its normal crack of sound. Not knowing why. Just sensing that it should not.

She went down the steps and across the yard, making her feet firm upon the place where she had fallen in the dark, because this was home and it must not be haunted. One had to live here.

The stable door was open. She looked in. He had his back to her.

'Dad?'

He turned a face of terror. She felt as if he had hit her, so strongly did he will her to come no nearer. Her heart began to race.

'What's the matter?' she said.

'No, no,' he said. 'It's nothing. Don't think about it. I'll see that you're not bothered. I'll see to that.' His pale blue eyes had a look she had never seen in them before.

'What am I not supposed to think about?' she asked.

'No, I can't,' he said. 'It's insane. Insane. He can't know what he is saying or doing. I told poor Abby.'

Felicia, her mind flashing back to Saturday night, put both hands on the door jamb and cried out, 'Dad, I haven't done anything wrong! I haven't! I swear it!'

'I know,' he groaned, 'I know. And neither have I—that I knew or intended. I wish— I have to think, you know. But there's the question. Where to turn to get the money. I was thinking of boarding school . . .'

Then, as if he couldn't look at her any longer, he turned towards the big window, his face and his throat working.

'You won't believe *a lie!*' she cried.

'No, no,' he said, 'no, no, no. Or I could sell all this. I suppose . . . I suppose . . .'

She knew him so well. He wasn't believing a lie. No, something had hurt him and frightened him more terribly than she had ever seen him hurt or frightened. All she wanted to do, in this or any other world, was to run to him, touch him, send from her own frightened heart the strong and ancient messages of love, of loyalty, of her simple presence for his comfort. She ran two steps and then he turned and stopped her with that look of anguished fear. No, better not? Must not?

'It's all right,' he said falsely, with his poor

136

smile, his poor, put-on painful smile. 'We won't let it destroy us. I don't want you to think about it. I will take care of you. I will think of the way. People are not as cruel as that. Just let me alone to think of something, will you, darling?' Her father was weeping. 'Just be a good girl?'

Felicia said, in a little girl's voice, 'Daddy, if I fix a sandwich for lunch, will that be all right?'

'All right,' he groaned. He buckled. He sat on a box. 'I wish . . . I wish . . . your mother . . . wish your mother were alive.'

But she is not, Felica thought. Death took her. Old Brother Death. We are the ones who are alive. That is the hard thing.

What was destroying him? He had his conscience, so vulnerable, so dainty, that he had never carved the Tiki-god. His ways went down the charming by-paths; the small enchantments were his concern. He saw no evil. He had his stubborn values, and his standards, and so his goodness. He had ever been her loving father and she loved him but . . .

She was very, very old and she had seen much evil. She could do nothing for him. Not now. It was sad. It was hard. It was true.

She would be a good girl and leave him alone.

*   *   *

When she came into the house, the phone was ringing. 'Is this the . . . little Lorimer girl?

'Yes.'

'Is your father there, dear?'

'Yes, but . . .'

'May I speak to him?' The woman's voice was timid and very sweet.

'Not now. I'm sorry,' Felicia said.

'This is Mrs. George Harper.' The voice went up to question recognition.

'Yes, Mrs. Harper?'

'Mr. Harper and I would like very much for you to come and stay with us a little while. Will you do that?' The voice seemed to assume that Felicia was about twelve years old.

'I don't know you,' Felicia said, bewildered.

'Mr. Harper and I thought perhaps you would rather come and stay with people you don't know.'

'Why?'

'This whole thing is . . . so unfortunate. Mr. Harper and I are afraid that the story is going to get around. We . . . we'—the woman was getting breathless—'only want to try to do what is fair. Mr. Harper regrets the whole thing and so do I, of course. We feel that we . . . Couldn't I speak to your father?'

'No,' said Felicia. 'What story?'

'Oh!' It was a little yelp of consternation.

'I'd like to know just how . . . it was put to you,' said Felicia craftily.

138

'But surely, if you . . . It's just not wise, right now, dear, for you to stay alone in that house.' The woman was agitated.

'I don't stay here alone,' said Felicia loudly. 'I live here with my father.'

The woman's breath gasped in. Felicia, connected with that gasp of air, was suddenly connected with the nature of the lie. 'Disgusting old beast,' 'Terrible business,' 'Not wise to stay alone in that house *with your father . . .*'

She heard the woman wail, 'George, I can't talk to her. You'll have to do it.'

A man said, 'Hallo? Hallo?'

She didn't speak, but she didn't hang up.

'Little girl? Listen, we are coming right over.'

'No.'

'These damn' women are going to spread this thing all over town and it's not going to be any fun a-*tall*. Now, we only want to help you . . . and I don't care what the truth is—'

'You can't help me,' Felicia said. She hung up. She ran upstairs.

*   *   *

Nearly noon, and Cleona put her head out of the kitchen door of the Cunningham-Crown house and said, 'Hi, Miss Felicia. Was that you rattling the pool gate?'

'I guess it was.' The girl just stood there,

139

looking behind her.

'I'm waiting on the doctor.' Cleona let her ample form out through the screen door. 'Or either Mr. Crown, when he gets the message.' Cleona felt like talking out the pressures of her responsibility. 'Miss Abigail, she don't feel so good.'

'Poor Abby?' the girl said. She had on a blue cotton shirt and skirt. She looked too dressed up for a summer noon and yet not dressed up enough.

'Oh, I got her quiet now,' Cleona said fanning herself. 'Her and Mr. Ladd had some words, I think that's it.'

'Mr. Ladd Cunningham? He isn't here?'

'No, ma'am. But you all want to go swimming, Miss Felicia, you know where the key is at. Sure is hot in the sun.'

'It would be cool,' said Felicia, 'in the water.' Cleona now gave her a sharp look. 'Where you going, child, with that big old suitcase? You don't look like you feel so good yourself.'

'I was in a hurry.' Felicia pushed at her hair and looked behind her again.

'You all visiting some friend of yours? Over night, probably?' The girl had her good shoes on but her hair was tied up, any old way, in a rubber band. Cleona was puzzled.

'Yes, over the night.'

'One of them slumber parties?' Cleona hooted. 'And nobody sleeps a wink?'

Felicia said, 'Is it lonelier in Liverpool? Do

140

you super-suffer in Saskatchewan?'

'What's that?'

'Nothing. Just silly. Silly, Cleona. Tell Mr. and Mrs. Harper—'

'I don't know any Mr. and Mrs. Harper.'

'Neither do I.'

Cleona said, 'You all come in here and let me give you a cool drink. You hear?'

But Felicia braced herself and smiled up at the black woman. 'I liked Mr. Hob Cunningham, didn't you?'

'I sure did. But Mr. David Crown, he is a very nice gentleman, too.'

'So was my father.'

'Yes, ma'am.'

'Good-bye, Cleona.'

'You all have fun, hear?'

Cleona shaded her eyes to watch the girl trudge down the Cunningham drive to the Cunninghams' street. Then Cleona saw the doctor's handsome automobile swoop to the kerb and she smoothed her apron and her uniform and ducked back through the house to open the front door.

CHAPTER TEN

'She's quiet, Mr. Crown. Dr. Jones, he's up there now. She didn't have no accident or anything. Her and Mr. Ladd had some words;

141

that was it. And Dr. Jones, he's taking care.'

'Good. Thank you, Cleona. Where is Mr. Ladd now?'

'Oh, he gone. He took off in his automobile.'

'I see.'

David felt no surprise. He felt, in fact, relief, believing that things were coming to a head in this house, the trouble would be opened up. He looked into Cleona's beautiful mahogany-coloured eyes, feeling, as he often had, that she was a wise woman. 'Do you know what happened?'

'No, sir, I doesn't,' said Cleona, 'but Mr. Ladd, *he* ain't been feeling too right with himself for a long time.'

'I agree with you.' David started for the stairs and saw Dr. Jones coming down.

Cleona was two jumps ahead of his thought. 'I'll go be with her,' she said and passed the doctor on the stairs.

'Mr. Crown? She's all right.'

'Good. Will you come in here a minute?'

'Certainly.'

They went into the library. David did not know this doctor at all. He was Abby's doctor. He had not been Hob's. He was a little slick for David's taste and a little too prosperous-looking. 'What is it?' David asked him bluntly.

'Emotion,' said Dr. Jones. He sat down in one of the leather chairs, evidently not worried about any dying person to whom he owed a

142

visit, or, for any other reason, on tenterhooks to be off.

David offered him a cigarette which the doctor took.

'Abby is very high-strung,' the doctor said, 'It doesn't take much to set her off.'

'Do you know what "set her off"?' said David stiffly.

'No, no. I believe that certain things were said that hurt her feelings in some way. She seems worried about her son.'

'Rightly so,' said David. He did not know this man. He did not know how far he wanted to venture into confidence with him.

'I don't know the boy,' said the doctor, flicking his lighter shut. 'But it is too bad that Abby can't be protected from this sort of thing. Oh, she'll be all right. Physically, you know, there's not much wrong with her.'

'Then these spells of what you call "emotion" are not dangerous to her?' said David flatly. He did not like something here that began to sound two-faced.

The doctor was evasive. 'Why, not this one. But of course a chronic state of high emotion isn't good for anyone.' Very smooth.

David said, 'There is something I must ask you. What did you prescribe for Abby in the way of pills for pain?'

'For pain?'

'Last summer.'

'Last summer?' The doctor's brows went up.

'May I ask why you ask?'

'Yes. Abby tells me she had some pills for pain and she took them to her husband in the hospital.'

'Oh,' said Dr. Jones, 'those.'

'Were they dangerous?'

'Dangerous?' The doctor cocked his head and looked amused. 'Well, I don't suppose that if you were to swallow them down by the handful that they would do you any particular good. However, I don't order very strong drugs for Abby. The suggestion is often enough.'

Again David had the sense of treachery. 'Could they have killed him?' David was sharp.

'Killed whom?' The doctor was jolted upright.

'Hob Cunningham, if he took them all?'

'But he didn't.'

'Didn't?'

'Not those pills. As a matter of fact, those pills are kicking around my office, somewhere, to this very day.'

'*You* have them?'

'Oh, yes.'

'But how?'

'Why, I had a patient in the hospital, as I remember, on the same floor with Mr. Cunningham, and the nurse spoke to me. She showed me my own prescription, written for Abby, and wanted to know what to do with those pills.'

'I see. Then they were found. When?'

'I can't give you the day.'

'Before Hob died?'

'I suppose so. I think so. What difference? He certainly didn't take them. *I* took them. That is, I put them in my pocket and promised to get them back to Abby. But somehow or other, whenever I had the chance I managed to forget. I knew, you see, that she had wanted to be helpful. It was her little sacrifice. I hated to . . . Well, let's just leave it that I never did give them back to her. They are not . . . expensive.' And anyhow, Abby Cunningham could afford the loss. The implication hung in the air.

David sank back into his own chair. 'I wonder if there was any time . . . Was this before Thanksgiving, do you know?'

Dr. Jones shook his head. He did not know. He was wary, now.

'I am wondering if the boy had seen those pills in his father's room.'

'The boy?'

'Yes. You see, he thinks his father was poisoned.'

'Does he indeed?' said the doctor thoughtfully. 'But Abby doesn't know that?'

'No.'

'Then you should tell her.'

'I should?'

'Yes, I think so. She needs . . .'

'What?'

'Well, a rationale.'

145

'For the boy's behaviour?'

'That's it.'

'I see.'

Now Dr. Jones smiled. 'I am primarily concerned for *my* patient,' he explained with charm.

'Yes. Well, then, I'll go up. Thank you.'

They shook hands. Then the doctor said smoothly, 'These super-sensitive people, you know, have a much more difficult time of it than those of us whose skins are thicker. Is the boy, perhaps, a little like his mother?'

'Perhaps,' said David guardedly.

As he went upstairs David was thinking to himself, I do not like thee, Dr. Fell.

*   *   *

Abby was lying quietly upon her bed, not truly in it, wearing one of her pretty dressing-gowns, with a soft 'throw' over her feet. Cleona melted away like a fat shadow. David sat down on the bed's edge and took his wife's hand. 'Well?' he said, smiling.

'I am sorry, David. I frightened myself, I felt so . . .'

'But you are better?'

'Oh, much,' she said without enthusiasm.

'Do you want to talk? Or would you rather not?'

'I don't know. Where is he?'

'Cleona says he went off in his car.'

146

'Yes.' Abby rolled her head. She was not stupid. She was perhaps frail of her very lack of stupidity. 'It worries me,' she said. 'It worries me.'

'Abby dear, I'll have to tell you something. Please listen.' (Her eyes came to his begging this not to be bad news, not to be terrible.) 'It is Ladd who had got it into his head that Hob was poisoned. Ladd was the one who called the policeman on the phone.'

Her flesh seemed to fall backward and downward from the prow of her dainty nose. Her eyes widened slowly. 'How could he?'

'I don't know, dear. But I've just talked to Dr. Jones about your famous pills. And there is nothing to worry about on that score.' He told her what had happened to her pills and Abby sighed. The colour crept a little higher on her delicate skin.

She popped up on one elbow. 'Oh. Do you think Ladd could have seen them in Hob's room?'

'He may have.'

'Oh . . . and then he thought . . .' Her eyes fled. 'But oh, why'—she sank back—'why didn't he come to me when he first . . . ?'

(Because you couldn't bear it, thought David.) 'Because he loves you,' said David lightly, 'for one reason.'

Abby flushed and struggled higher against her pillows. 'I wonder. I wonder. The policeman said that the phone call said that

147

you had done it. But do you suppose Ladd thinks . . . ?'

'That we both did?' David finished for her.

'But then,' she cried, almost in delight, 'We must find him! And the sooner we find him the sooner we can explain. And the sooner he will be rid of that terrible thought! Oh, my poor baby!' There was something a little false in her joy.

'I don't quite know how to find him, Abby. He's riding around, or at the beach, or with some friend. It's a big city.'

'He'll be home for dinner,' Abby said, with an absurd confidence. She let herself slowly sink into the pillows, and turned one cheek against the linen.

'Do you want to tell me,' said David in a moment, 'what Ladd did or said?'

'I don't think so,' she said drearily. 'I don't want to quote him, especially. I don't know that I could. But now that I understand how he has been troubled . . . And then there's been some involvement with Felicia Lorimer.'

'What?'

'Oh, some romantic skirmish. I'm not sure. He didn't really know, at all, what he was saying. So I don't suppose he will remember. Maybe it is better if he never does remember.'

'Will you sleep now?' David kissed her soft cheek. She did not move her head. She looked at the lamp and said, 'David, do you think Aaron Silver would talk to Ladd?'

148

(Oh, Abby, inconsistent!)

'I'm sure that Aaron would. I'm not sure that Ladd would let him,' David said honestly.

She rolled her head. 'I don't think so,' she said, as if it had been his proposal. 'I think when we explain, *he'll* be all right.'

'We'll see,' said David. He patted her and started away.

As he got to the door she said in a low voice, 'David, don't leave me.'

'No, no.'

'I mean, now,' she said. 'Don't go anywhere.'

'All right—except down to beg some lunch from Cleona.'

'All right, darling.'

She fluttered to repose.

David went away.

His confidence that they had reached an understanding, even if obliquely, was wavering a little. Was Abby satisfied, or determined to think that reason could reach the boy and heal everything? David was not sure. And was she determined, with all her power, to 'forgive and forget?' David was not so sure of that, either. Something in a pronoun . . .

What the devil kind of scene had the kid made? he wondered. And where the devil is he? And what the devil am I going to do? He went downstairs, pondering his dilemma, which existed just as it had before.

David spoke to Cleona (who was one jump

ahead of him) about lunch. Then he called the Fenwick house. There was no answer. He was flipping through the pages of the little book of handy phone numbers wondering where next, what friends, to call, when Cleona announced his meal.

No person had yet told David Crown that Rafe Lorimer had been in the house during the morning or involved in any way. So the Lorimers were not pertinent in his thoughts. He had made nothing of Abby's remark about Felicia. He was mildly surprised when Cleona mentioned the girl.

'Miss Felicia Lorimer came by, Mr. Crown, a while back.'

'Oh?'

'She don't look like *she* feels so good.'

'That's too bad.'

'She knows where the key is at.'

'Then what?'

'The key to the swimming pool.'

'Yes, of course she does. The Lorimer kids are always in and out. Did she want to go swimming?'

'I don't know did she or didn't she,' Cleona said.

'Well, if she went by, then she didn't.' He smiled at her.

'She going to some slumber party. She talked so silly! Head nor tail, to me.'

Cleona's eyes were trying to say more than her mouth said but David was attacking his

150

plate, anxious to get back to his own problem. He said carelessly, 'Some of these kids speak a language all their own.'

'Yes, sir.'

*   *   *

When he had eaten, David went into the library and did what he knew he ought to do. He called Dr. Silver. Dr. Silver was not in. He called the Fenwick house again. No answer.

He called the plant to say that he would not be back. Some business calls ensued.

Then it was two o'clock. Abby was asleep. Cleona kept to her own part of the house. David, knowing no way to find Ladd Cunningham, gave up telephoning, went out upon the terrace, and settled himself. It was a bright hot day. The pool was very pretty, lying unruffled in the sunshine. David considered, lazily, the prospect of getting himself into a pair of trunks and splashing about. But he did not. He was a clumsy swimmer. He had not been in the pool much. It was for the young.

He lay back in a long chair, cool enough, comfortable. Everything was quiet. He could see the roof of Rafe's studio, the upper part of the Lorimer house, glimmering pale through green trees. Nothing stirred there.

This was Hob Cunnigham's place, Hob's castle. David thought, I ought to take my wife and move away.

151

He thought, with longing, of his own girls. Skinny, long-legged Angie, so full of mischief —slangy and quick—being a young mother now. And Patty, so full of ambition and young grace and young pride. He thought of June, who never had had two cents' worth of pity for herself. And it is well known, he thought, that kids don't learn through precepts but through their pores.

Wait. Hold it. Too easy to visit the sins of the children upon their parents. Too simple to be true. If he was the reasonable, the honest, the examining man, then he had better hold it a minute and think twice. Soberly and fairly, he considered Abby, who was not June, and not anybody else but Abby. Poor Abby. Whatever she knew or guessed or merely sensed—which he quietly conceded to be, under Abby's mixture, probably everything— the fact was that Abby was being tortured. And it would have to be stopped.

But how?

CHAPTER ELEVEN

Rafe Lorimer sat on the box with his head in his hands, trying to think. He'd raise some money. He'd raise hell with the Cunningham boy. He'd go there. He'd— But he knew that Abby was in one of her twits right now, and had the doctor coming. No use trying to raise hell with Abby. He'd get hold of that damnable boy. Who was mad. For surely, to destroy, for the sake of destroying, was madness. What use trying to raise hell with such a boy? Then he'd raise all the devils of hell with David Crown. With someone. With them all.

But not until he felt cooler and steadier. No. Rafe had a vision of himself, foolish and furious, sputtering without plan, in no direction, making no impression. No, no, I must be composed. I must know exactly what I am going to say. I must have my dignity back. (But oh, never my little daughter!) He wept. I will have to tell her, he wept. She can't be left ignorant. Oh God, I will have to tell her and then . . . ?

His hands moved of themselves. Laid out on a kind of taboret were his tools, and his hands went to them. He shifted his rump. The block of wood stood on the floor. There had been a vision in it. He had worked off one upper corner. The curve of the skull of the head of the vision was invisible but it was there; he had begun to let it out. His eyes were tearful. He could scarcely see, but the knife jumped into his hand. His hand went to work. The work went of itself. His tears dried. His mind began to settle.

When Mr. and Mrs. George Harper came, calling his name, to the studio door, Rafe was

153

in his own world again.

'Your daughter doesn't answer the door-bell.'

'Why should she?' Rafe said. He went on to say that she had her rights. The house was her house and her home. If she did not wish to receive callers, she need not. As for going to stay with them, that, too, was Felicia's choice. She had said not? Then, not.

Mrs. Harper was a little woman, timid and faded. She watched him fearfully. 'No, I am not a monster,' Rafe told her in a kindly aside.

But what was he going to do? They wanted to know.

Obviously, Rafe told them, he was going to have to sue. Mrs. Harper moaned. 'But I must,' Rafe said. 'Not for my own sake. I have my work. I don't need anything else. I have never cared, and never will care, what people say. The worse for them if they believe a lie.'

'But the little girl,' moaned Mrs. Harper. 'Her whole life . . .'

'I shall send Felicia abroad to school,' said Rafe. 'Switzerland, or perhaps France. She is not an ordinary child, in any case.' He could see her in this vision, becoming an artist perhaps. Shaking off this cramped provincial atmosphere. He would wrest good from evil and set her free.

Mrs. Harper said, 'Mr. Lorimer, you should stop and think. You oughtn't to make it a public scandal.'

'I didn't choose to have a scandal at all.'

Old Mr. Harper said, 'You've told the little girl, have you, what the young fellow said?'

'No, no. Not yet. But I shall. Then I shall go to the Cunninghams. A litte later, when they are all there.' He lied to excuse his delay. 'I'll sue the boy and them, through him. They have plenty of money. That boy's insane malice will have to be paid for.'

'Money, eh?' Old Mr. Harper bristled up.

'I have no money,' Rafe explained patiently. 'It will take a good deal of money to send Felicia abroad to live.' His voice trembled a little because, even in this fine vision, he'd lost his daughter.

Mr. Harper pursed his lips and nodded. But Mrs. Harper was trembling, all over. 'Wouldn't it be better to let it go? Ignore it? Don't do this. Mr. Harper and I will never say a word.'

Mr. Harper said morosely, 'I dunno how you are going to keep Elsie Marshall quiet.'

'Then I shall sue Elsie Marshall, too,' said Rafe, smiling. 'Thank you for coming.' The old pair seemed to be swept out of his studio by the broom of his grand resolve.

Rafe puttered a moment, but his concentration had been broken. It was late. He went into the house after some lunch. A note on the kitchen table. *Dad: S. in wax paper in ice-box.*

Rafe found his sandwich and poured a glass of milk. The house was quiet. He thought that

155

Felicia must be lying low because of the Harpers. He went into the hall and called her name, not very loudly. She didn't answer. Rafe took breath to call again and his heart quailed. He would have to tell her. But oh, not yet. Not this minute. Let her have a quarter of an hour more of innocent peace. He went back to the kitchen and ate his sandwich, drank his milk.

*   *   *

In their car, the Harpers were headed for home. Old Mrs. Harper could feel the aching in her bones subsiding, for she had ached, anticipating a young person in their house and their carefully studied and suitable routine all knocked to pieces. 'We did our best,' she said.

Old Mr. Harper was thinking of something else. 'I suppose if he does go to law, that I got to be a witness.' He pursed his mouth. 'All I can say is, if that boy's a liar, he's a darned good one. To fool *me*! Not going to be any fun a-*tall* to get up and have to repeat that dirty stuff.'

'We did all we could,' his wife said, with mournful satisfaction. But Mr. Harper began to rub his chest with the heel of his hand. The car wavered and slowed.

'Daddy?' she said in a little thin voice.

*   *   *

156

Rafe wandered to and fro in the kitchen. The Cunninghams now? No, not yet. Not quite yet. Taking no thought, he went by habit out to his studio. He sat down on the box. He was thinking about a law-suit. For slander, is it? Or libel? He didn't even know the terms. A lawyer, then. Court. Judge. Testimony. The old lady had reminded him of publicity. Would he have to talk to reporters? How could Rafe deal with all these unaccustomed bustling affairs? All he wanted was to work, just quietly, where he was. Bearing no ill will to anyone. Not bothering or being bothered. He didn't understand the procedures. He didn't know the steps to take or what would be required of him during the next step and the step after that. He would need someone to help him through it all. Someone . . .

Then Rafe thought of his son. Justin, the cool and the bright. A piercing fear nailed him to the box. He could not move.

No, he would have to think this out very carefully. He mustn't make a mistake. The old lady might be right. Perhaps he should rise above the whole nasty business.

*　　　*　　　*

David, restless, as the afternoon wore on, called Dr. Silver again. Dr. Silver was still out, very sorry. Oh yes, Mr. Crown's calls were noted.

157

It was late afternoon when at last David got an answer at the Fenwick number, from Gary himself, who had been over to the college registering, who hadn't seen Ladd today, did not know where he was, could not usefully guess, could not suggest anyone who might know. But, sure thing, yes, sir, he'd come over.

*   *   *

Gary, being 'over,' was at first a lump.

Abby was dressing now to come down for dinner. David felt he had no time to waste on being wily.

'You and Ladd, between you, cooked up that phone call to your uncle?'

'I don't know what you're talking about, sir.'

'Ladd thinks that his father was killed?'

'I don't know, sir.'

'Why does he think so?'

'I don't know, sir.' Then Gary, his big hands clenching, added, 'But Uncle Walt is going to check up on that and so . . .'

'So?' David waited.

'So that's okay.'

'Yes, that's okay. I think your uncle is a good man.'

'Yes, sir.' Gary began to relax a little.

'What I need to know,' said David candidly, throwing out candour in faith (or for bait?), 'is this. Does Ladd really believe that I killed his sick father? Or was he simply threshing

158

around, to cause trouble, because he doesn't like me?'

'I don't know, sir,' Gary looked up. 'Honest.' The round eyes in the fleshy face were honest, now. And troubled, too. 'He . . .'

'Yes?'

'. . . doesn't like you too much.'

'I've been well aware of that,' said David gravely. 'I've tried very hard to like him. He doesn't help much.'

'No, sir,' Gary mumbled.

'Can you think of anything that I can do?'

'No, sir,' Gary's head was down.

'I realise,' said David, 'that I am embarrassing you. I'm sorry. But I'm in a mood to try anything. I would imagine that you'd like to see him a little . . . lighter-hearted than he has been lately?'

'He's my best friend.'

'I know.' David waited.

'I guess you couldn't go away,' the boy mumbled.

'Go away? Is that it?' David pounced.

'Well, he . . . did say he'd like to . . .'

'Yes?'

'. . . get rid of you,' burst Gary. 'He doesn't mean anything too bad.' The big lad squirmed. 'He's my best friend.'

David said kindly, 'All right. Thank you.'

'That's okay,' Gary said, but now that he was dismissed he lingered. 'Look, Mr. Crown, there isn't anything to worry about. Nothing's

159

going to happen. I mean, my Uncle Walt isn't anybody's fool.'

'Let's hope,' said David sadly, 'that none of us is going to be anybody's fool.'

*   *   *

When Gary had gone, David called the Detective Bureau and asked for Walter Douglas.

'Well, sir, that looks like a tangent, all right,' Douglas said, after listening to the whole tale of Abby's pills. 'By the way, Mr. Cunningham's doctor, and all the hospital personnel that I could find to talk to, never had any doubt about him. No poison symptoms. Said his heart gave out with the stress of the other thing. So there's nothing in it.'

'Still, the boy may believe that there's something in it. He took off in his car just before noon—I think it was—and we don't know where he is. He may have been in an emotional state. He had a run-in of some kind with his mother and she is . . . very much worried. Is there any way—'

'To pick him up?' said Douglas promptly. 'That's not my division. but *I'd* say no, there is not. Not simply because his mother is worried about him.'

'I see that. But in this case she—and I—may be rightfully worried.'

'Well,' said the policeman, 'if he gets into

any trouble . . .'

'Worse before treatment?'

'What's that?'

'I'm anxious to find him before there is any trouble.'

'Yes, well . . . What does he drive?'

'A Corvette. Convertible.'

'Year? Colour?'

'Nineteen sixty-one. Blue.'

'Know the licence?'

'Afraid not.'

'Well, sir, I'll . . . uh . . . keep this on hand. One thing—you might look over any snapshots he's got.'

'Snapshots?'

'People take pictures of new cars, or even old ones. Sometimes the licence number shows up.'

'I see. All right, I'll try.' Then David added, a little bitterly, 'It will give me something to do, won't it?'

Gary's uncle said, 'That's right.'

David hung up, thinking of the boy in the car, somewhere in the great complex of the city of Los Angeles and all its suburbs. Where anything could be found. Sea, mountains, desert, what'll you have? Slums and alleys. Posh palaces of the rich. Hundred of miles of the decent dwellings of decent folks. Or any kind of folks. Drink, dope and depravity, or the noble arts and sciences. And everything in between. Now come . . . not everything is equally probable. David was, somehow, inclined to imagine the boy on a beach. But there were a hundred miles of beach.

David sighed and went upstairs and along the wing to the boy's room. The door was closed and he felt a great reluctance to open it. He had never yet been through this door.

But he opened it. The room seemed pitiful to him. So young. So young. The low-slung furniture. The trappings. He did not want to touch anything. He sent his eyes searching for an album, a box, somewhere the boy would keep snapshots. He saw no such thing.

He did not want to rummage through drawers and cupboards. The low bed had a headboard of shelves with books and papers haphazard upon them. David went to peer at these. He put one hand on the pillow to lean to look at the shelves on the far side. His hand felt something hard.

What . . .? He took his hands off, feeling guilty. Then he plucked at the spread and turned it back. He shifted the pillow. There was a stone under the pillow. A stone of the size to fit the palm of the hand.

David had seen this stone before. Hob Cunningham used to keep it on his desk, for some unknown reason. David felt a sting behind his eyes. So pitiful! He put the pillow and the spread back into place. He looked around the room once more. He hurried out of it.

He had intruded.

*   *   *

Downstairs, in the library, Abby was on the telephone.

'Thank you so much for calling. We were worried, but I really think, don't you, that once we get this frightful idea out of his . . .' She saw David come in. 'Oh, David. It's Aaron. But I've told him . . .'

David came near and took the phone, warm from her hand.

'Aaron?'

'Sorry I was tied up all day. Abby says the boy thinks there was something "funny" about Hob's dying! Is that so?'

'Seems so.'

'Seems, eh? What do you want me to do, Dave?'

'Talk to him.' David could see Abby's face and its distress. 'Is that a good idea?'

'For me to talk to him? Depends. Get him to my office?'

'I don't know whether I can.'

'Shall I give you a name or two? Somebody else might be better. I told you.'

'Somebody else,' said David, 'also suggested by me?'

'Well, there is that. Do you think he realises now that he needs some help?'

'I don't know. He isn't here.'

'If he doesn't,' said Aaron, 'I thought I told you. We do not come in the white coats with the butterfly nets.'

Not until too late, eh? thought David grimly. He did not say it. Abby was there.

Aaron said, 'Talk to him yourself. Persuade him, if you can.'

'I can only try. Thanks, Aaron. We'll see how it is.' He hung up and Abby smiled at him.

He heard Rafe Lorimer say, 'David, I must talk to you alone.'

CHAPTER TWELVE

Rafe had come in unannounced. There he was, in the door to the hall, in his old clothes, his sandals, with his hair on end as it ever was. But he was not smiling any kind of smile. He had an air of exhaustion. He looked like a man who had come to the end of his rope.

Abby's hands were at her throat. 'Oh, Rafe, what is it?'

Rafe did not even look at her. David moved quickly. This time it was bad. He knew that. He took Abby by her elbows. 'Darling, if Rafe says he wants to talk to me alone?' He spoke to her gently, but he challenged her manners.

Abby's eyes winced, her lids fluttered. 'Yes, of course,' she said. 'I'm sorry.' He moved her by a gentle pressure towards the door to the

164

living-room. She kept her frightened eyes on his face, begging him. David, don't let it be anything terrible. Don't let it be anything that I cannot bear.

David closed the door behind her. 'All right, Rafe. What is it?'

Rafe told him what it was.

*　　　*　　　*

Her little note was pitiful. Pitiful. Rafe had finally found it, pinned to her pillow. *Daddy: I'm going away by myself for a couple of days. You know I have to.*

Rafe, huddled in a chair, his eyes red-rimmed, said, 'I was ready to try to ignore that cruel and crazy episode—just live it down for a lie. But not now. I don't know how she heard it but she knows what that wicked boy is saying. So listen to me, David. Somebody has got to listen. She's seventeen years old; she's never been away from her home. She has no money. Understand that? Listen to it! No money. Where has she gone?' Rafe's voice was rising. 'Where is my little girl? He has driven her out of her home, don't you see that? Away from her rightful protection. He's dirtied her whole world and broken her life and driven her out and all for no reason. No reason. I have to find her. Now. Tonight. This is my *child*! I won't have her driven away. And then I am going to law about this. Going to sue that boy and Abby and you and anybody else . . . not for the money but for some justice here.' Rafe's voice was going into a ranting spiral. He was like a man in a cage. 'But I'll take some money, because she must have this made up to her. Do you understand that? She must have a *better* chance than before. I want to send her to Europe to school. Set her free, with advantages. Set her free. But not all alone and without any money in this terrible city . . . by herself.' Now, Rafe wept openly.

David said quietly, 'We'll find her.' He would not minimise the trouble of this big sloppy dishevelled man, more than sixty years old, weeping in the chair. He would not give false comfort. He said, 'Rafe, if Ladd did this to you, then you must sue, if you want to sue, and you will win. You needn't do it for the money. Anything, in the way of money, to send Felicia to any school in the world, you'll have. I'll see to that. And as for justice, I'll go with you to see this Mr. Harper and those women, every one of them. If Ladd did this to you, then I will tell them that the boy is disturbed, that he lied in his sickness, that there is no truth in him. Everything I can possibly do to *undo* this, believe me, Rafe, I will do.'

'And can you tell me where she is now? Can you tell me that?'

'I can go with you now,' said David. 'We can search for her. I'll take you. I'll do what I can.'

But Rafe huddled in the chair and falling,

166

falling into the strange cushiony lack of any resistance at all, said sadly, 'Can you give me back my little daughter . . . as we were?'

David felt sick at this question because the answer was No.

'You can't,' said Rafe, with sad, exhausted dignity, 'put Humpty-Dumpty together again.'

David got up, every trained cell responding to a discipline. One did what one could. 'Have you called the police, Rafe?'

'Yes. Yes.'

'What did they say?'

'They said I must come in and make out a report.'

'Then we'll do that. I'll take you. Have you a list of her friends?'

'I've phoned them.'

'All of them?'

'All I know. All I know. What do I know? She hasn't many friends. She was a home-loving child.' Rafe was going to weep again.

'Wait a minute,' said David. 'It seems to me . . . Cleona saw her.'

'Cleona?'

David started for the door.

Rafe said, 'I don't want to see Abby. I won't see Abby. I'm going to leave her to you. And the boy, too. I can't see either of them.'

'That's all right. Sit here, Rafe. We'll go in a minute.' David left the room.

Rafe sat in the chair and let himself fall. He should have come to David Crown at once, at once—much sooner. David was a man of affairs, like Hob Cunningham. David was strong within the main currents. No putterer. No bungling incompetent. *He'll* find her, Rafe told himself with sudden hope. And all this, all this, will pass like a very bad dream.

*　　　*　　　*

Cleona's eyes rolled. She cried out, 'Something happen to that child!'

'Why do you say that?' David spoke quietly. They were in the kitchen. Abby was in the living-room. 'She talk so silly. Worried me.'

'What did she say?'

'Too silly to remember.'

'She came along our driveway?'

'Yes, sir. Yes, sir. Went ahead on down the street. She had a big old suitcase she was dragging.'

'A suitcase?' David pounced. 'And wait . . . didn't you say something earlier, about a party?'

'Yes, sir, Mr. David, that's what I said. But I can't remember did she say Yes, she was or No, she wasn't.'

'Going to a party?'

'A slumber party,' Cleona said. Her eyes rolled.

'Something happen to that child?' she whimpered.

David touched her arm and steadied her.

168

'The suitcase is hopeful,' he said grimly.

'Oh, I remember— She do speak like her daddy was dead.'

'Dead!'

'Something happen to Mr. Rafe Lorimer?'

'No, no. He's here. Mr. Rafe and I are going out to see what we can do. You must stay with Miss Abby.'

'Yes, sir, but Miss Abby, she going to carry on.' Cleona looked frightened.

'I am going to tell her,' said David clearly, 'that Miss Felicia has run away and Mr. Rafe wants her found. That's simple enough. Better not mention that you saw her at all. Try not to talk about it.'

'Yes, sir. No, sir.'

'Don't leave Miss Abby. Even if Mr. Ladd comes home, just do not leave her for anything until I come back.'

'No, sir, I ain't going to leave her,' Cleona said. 'Mr. David, don't you let something happen to that child.'

*   *   *

David went to pick up his car keys from the table in the hall and crossed into the big living-room where Abby sat with a white shawl around her summer dress. He thought, I must go with this man. But if I tell Abby the whole story, I cannot go. Therefore I will not tell her the whole story—yet. And that's what is simple enough.

So he told her that Felicia was missing, having run away, that he must take poor Rafe to look for her, that Abby must not wait dinner, she must stay quietly here with Cleona. And be all right?

Abby, big-eyed, shivered within the shawl.

*   *   *

When the men went out by the terrace door Rafe did not look into the room where she was or speak to her and Abby called out no word to him. Cleona came in and said, 'Miss Abby, you all want your dinner soon? Or you going to wait on Mr. Ladd?'

'I don't think Mr. Ladd will be here.' Abby touched her eyes with a corner of her shawl. 'It seems not. She really is a nice little thing, Cleona, and we do know her family. I'm sure it will work out, somehow. I don't know where they'd go. They are not of age. I suppose we'll have a telegram.'

Cleona looked stupid, which she was not, and said, 'Yes, ma'am.'

'So I'll tell you what.' Abby was suddenly gay. 'Set a place in the breakfast-room and, while I eat, you can talk to me.' Then Abby pulled her shawl tight. 'I'm lonely,' she said.

*   *   *

Rafe was borne comfortably, in David's car, to the police station. Rafe made out the paper in his own hand-writing as was required, and half attended to the rhythm of David's voice. (A man of affairs.) The police said they held a Missing Person report for twenty-four hours before acting, but David Crown was not having any of that.

'A seventeen-year-old girl who has no money?'

'Some of these seventeen-year-old chicks are pretty hep, Mr. Crown.'

'Not this one.' David was quietly stern. 'This one is rather a solitary little girl, and rather a sensitive one who has had a very bad blow. She is not the "hep chick" type and, even if she were, is in no state to be "hep" tonight. It is not a very good situation.'

'I see, Mr. Crown.'

'I really think you had better get on it.'

'I see, sir.'

Rafe, while he scribbled, did not catch all the overtones that flew above his tousled head. But they left with promises that the girl would be looked for, by all the resources of the department, and at once.

Rafe climbed back into the car and sighed heavily. He could never have accomplished that. He would have ranted or wept, and they would have put him down for hysterical. Sylvia, he thought, could have done it. But Sylvia was dead.

'We'll go to this Mr. Harper,' said David.

'Now?'

'Yes, because we are making an assumption here,' David said. 'Only Mr. Harper talked to the boy? You didn't see him?'

'No.'

'Did the ladies see him?'

'I don't know. They couldn't see out the south side of my studio. Maybe through the door.'

'We'll have to have Mr. Harper's, or somebody's identification.'

'It was Ladd Cunningham.' Rafe set his face stubbornly.

'I believe it,' David said, 'but we had better get Mr. Harper's description, at least. I need to talk to them, anyway.'

'But I don't know where they live,' cried Rafe, running into a blank . . . just as he had been thinking how brisk, how sensible, how orderly.

David Crown, it seemed, had ferreted the right Mr. Harper out of the phone book, somehow. All Rafe had to do was lean back.

But at the Harpers' little white cottage there was no answer to the bell, and no signs of life. A neighbour came down from his porch and told them, not without relish, that old Mr. Harper was in the hospital. A heart thing. So sudden! Of course, he was old. Oh yes, poor old Mrs. Harper was with him there. What the neighbour had heard, though, the old

172

fellow was going to 'get all right,' again. But one never knew, did one? That was life for you.

Back in the car, Rafe asked, 'To the hospital?'

'I don't think so,' said David gravely. 'Those poor people have had enough trouble for one day.'

'Oh, yes. Yes, of course.' Rafe felt shabby. He was also very weary. Tired of crisis. Tired of emotion. Tired of trouble. Tired of anger and of fear. He was an artist. He was accustomed to that detachment . . .

'This Elsie Marshall,' David said. 'What is her husband's name?'

'Oh, I know where she lives. On Hill Drive.'

'Hill Drive, then.'

Rafe could not stir his tired body or soul. He remained in the car while David went in to talk to Mrs. Marshall.

David came out and said, 'Well, I rather think the story has had some steam taken out of it.'

'How did you do it?' Rafe groaned.

'A dirty word, today,' said David, 'is "sheep." Which is to say "mob member" or "conformist." Mrs. Marshall will want to be on the "right" or individualistic, nonconforming, upright, and independently judging side. Oh, there is more than one way to put the ring in people's noses.'

'I don't understand you.'

'I don't wonder. I'm just blowing off. Being

cynical. Never mind. I fixed her. She didn't see the boy. Now we'll try the other two ladies. She told me where.'

So they called on the other two ladies, the one who had wanted to go home and was home, the other who had felt she ought to keep her mouth shut and was still saying so. David dealt with them, confirming them in their cowardice, bestowing upon them the good word 'maturity.' And that was that. Neither had seen the boy.

It was dark now. The night air was cool. Rafe was feeling numb and a little sleepy.

'Where shall I take you now, Rafe?' asked David obligingly.

'Take me home.'

'Are you sure?'

'Yes. Yes. She might even be there.'

'Yes, that is possible.'

So they came into the Cunningham drive and David ran his car into the garage, between Abby's car, and Hob's with its white cover— ghostly in the dark. He saw, with relief, that Ladd's little car was not under the carport.

So he guided Rafe through the gap in the hedge. The Lorimer house was dark. They went in together at the kitchen and Rafe turned up lights. David went with him all around the old house. Felicia's room was empty, silent, pitiful.

'I can't think . . .' said Rafe, and then with a new surge of panic, 'I can't *think*!'

174

'Don't think,' said David gently. 'The police will find her, you know. They can do it better than you and I.'

'I know.'

'I'd ask you to come to us for the night but—'

'No, no,' said Rafe, in terror. 'No, I must be here.' He had lost his daughter. He was alone. Well, then, alone. He needed nobody. Which was not a good kind loving thought but it came to him. He must be better than that. He must have faith, he must be very good and not get lost in his work but keep praying . . .

'She's been taken in,' said Rafe suddenly, 'by someone I simply haven't thought of.'

'I think that's very possible,' said David.

'David, how can I thank you?'

'Good night.' David wanted nobody's thanks for doing all that he could do, when he could not put Humpty-Dumpty together again.

He went back alone, through the hedge and along the driveway. The pool at his right caught the sky's light. He remembered something. He stopped beside the gate and he listened. There was no sound. The water was calm, as much as he could see of it. His heart shrank as he remembered how Cleona had said something, something about the pool, something doubtful.

David took the key out of its hiding place and unlocked the gate. He stepped fearfully within the enclosure and upon the concrete deck. The deep water was dark. Only the surface caught any light. He made his way to the pool house and found the switch for the underwater light. The big rectangle sprang into bright blueness. Nothing. Just the peaceful water, the main drain down there, a few brown leaves clinging at the curve of the walls.

He looked around the pool house, a structure with no front wall, built around Hob's barbecue, big fire-place, stone shelves. (Nobody used it now.) He looked into the two dressing-rooms, one at either side. There was nobody in the pool house.

David turned off the light and went slowly, in new darkness, to the gate. He locked it behind him. He put the key in his pocket. He went with a certain plodding, marching, stubborn step, up into the garden.

CHAPTER THIRTEEN

He was at the top of the four steps when light flooded the pavement below him. He heard the familiar engine sound, the drop and the new whine of acceleration. Ladd's blue Corvette, driven in Ladd's style, as individual as a signature, roared by towards the garages.

How dared he come waltzing blithely home! David went down the steps. Damned brat!

Selfish, destructive! Worthless little punk! I could kill him, thought David. Oh, I'll blast him. I'll pin him to the wall. I'll beat his ears off with the news of the evil he has done and the evil there is in his dirty little soul. And do it, here and now, where his mother cannot see or hear us when we clash under this sky and I put the fear of God into him!

Something made him look to his left. A police car, lights on its roof, had drifted parallel to the kerb, blocking the driveway. David turned to his left and hurried down the drive. The car awaited him. 'What is it?' he said in dread.

By the dashlight, he could see the round but rugged young face of the driver. 'Ladd Cunningham lives here, does he?'

'Yes. He does. What happened?'

'He was exceeding the speed limit on the Golden State, sir. Had to give him a citation.'

'Yes?'

'He co-operated.'

'I don't . . . understand.'

'He pulled over okay. He hasn't been drinking. He's not high. He told me that his father died. That so?'

'That's so.' (Yes, ten months ago.)

'Hard for a kid.' The cop himself was a kid to David's eye. 'You're related to him, sir?'

David nodded, still tense.

'Well, people will do that,' the young cop said. 'They get hit by a death in the family or a

177

girl turns them down or something. Kids especially, they'll go off and try to take their feelings out on a car. Well, I happened to be on my way—I mean coming off duty—and when he told me that, I didn't think he was in such a good state of mind to be on the roads at all. So I told him I'd dog him home, before something not-so-good happened.'

David stood, stunned.

'He made it fine. Drove real steady. Sorry about the citation. It'll go on his record. That can't be helped, sir.'

As his heart seemed to burst, expanding, David said 'Good for you' so vehemently that the young cop bridled with pleasure.

'Well, sir, then I guess you'll take care of him now?'

'Yes. Yes. Thanks.'

David went up the front walk, better balanced by an unexpected weight on the other side. His moment of pure rage had passed; his anger was tempered by mercy and good sense, for he had just seen these as facts, existing.

He let himself in at the front door of Hob Cunningham's house.

They were all three standing at the terrace end of the wide hall, Abby with her white shawl trailing, Cleona, and the boy. Abby's voice had a forced and feverish joy. 'Have you had anything to eat, dear?'

'Yes, thank you,' the boy said stiffly. He was

dishevelled. He was dirty.

Abby's eye had caught David's presence. 'Everyone is home now,' she said, on that same joyous note. 'Cleona, go to bed. You must be tired. Good night.'

Cleona caught David's nod (and the news of no success in his watchful austerity). She scuttled towards her quarters off the kitchen.

Now that the servant was gone, Abby said to her son in a little different tone, 'Oh, Ladd, my poor boy, you mustn't worry about it any more. I've been waiting to tell you. Your father never, never took those pills, dear. We know he didn't.'

David, not moving any closer, watched and listened. He could see that the boy was so physically tired that he could scarcely stand up.

'What pills?' said Ladd in a dull tone. 'I had to come home,' he said, stupidly. He was closed against her voice.

Abby stepped back and with one hand gathered up the trailing length of her shawl. 'And you *are* home, and I'm glad. We've been worried. A nice shower, dear?' She was too cheerful. 'And a good sleep? Shall I . . .?' She put out her other hand.

David said, 'Don't fuss, Abby. Let him be.' (He knew she mustn't touch.)

Ladd, with his rumpled jacket slung from a crooked forefinger over his shoulder, began to walk towards the foot of the stairs, and therefore towards David.

179

'Mr. Harper has had a heart attack,' said David quietly.

'Who?' the boy said. The dark eyes were wide open but in their depths they were closed.

'Felicia is missing.' Nothing moved in the dark eyes. 'Rafe Lorimer is frantic.' Nothing. Was there no getting through? 'You told a lie about them, didn't you?'

The eyes slitted. 'I'm not the liar.' Now there was a tension of resistance.

David did not touch him, either, although he had the impulse to do so—to assure him, to say to him, Don't be the way you are. So locked, so bitter, so haunted, so miserable. It isn't necessary. 'Will you go to see Dr. Silver, Ladd?' he asked.

'No.'

Abby had drawn closer. Her hand went out for David's support. He avoided her hand. She had better not touch either of them.

'Will you go to see some doctor? Any one you choose.'

The boy bent his head to the right and looked up, slyly. 'Maybe *you* need a doctor.' There was light in the slits of the eyes. 'Ever think of that?'

Abby shrank back.

'All right. Fair enough,' said David. 'If I go, will you go too?'

'No.' The boy was at bay, there at the foot of the stairs, facing the two of them. 'I want to go up to my room. May I?'

180

'Of course,' said Abby faintly.

But the boy said to David, in a furious snarl, '*May* I? *Sir?*'

David said nothing.

'You want to hit me. Why don't you hit me? I know you can't stand me around. You want to get rid of me? Hit me, then.'

Abby gasped. David, without a smile, just shook his head.

'*You* better go to your lousy Jew head-doctor,' the boy said bitterly, 'and you better be quick about it. I've had about as much as I can take.' He fled them, up the curve of the stairs.

*   *   *

They were sitting in the library, side by side. The door was closed. The big house was perfectly quiet. They had been speaking low, just the same.

Abby said, 'But was it Ladd? Are you sure?'

David said, 'I haven't been able to talk to Mr. Harper, but I am afraid it was, Abby. I am afraid so.' He had his arm behind her. He was waiting for the storm. It had not come yet.

'Oh, poor Rafe,' said Abby, almost in a whisper. 'I know what he must feel.'

'Felicia is probably quite all right.'

But Abby wasn't thinking of Felicia. 'Ladd was so furious with Rafe this morning.'

'What?'

'When Rafe was here. Didn't I say? I think Rafe had it in his mind to protect me. Ladd said some very nasty things. He called Rafe an old fool, and he said other things. Then he . . . just flung himself away.'

'That rather settles it,' said David sadly. He was waiting for her to cry.

'You knew all this when you went off?' said Abby.

'I was afraid to tell you,' he confessed.

'Then you don't . . . altogether understand.' Abby had the edge of her shawl in one hand. She rubbed her forehead with it. 'Oh, I'll fight . . . for nothing bad to happen. You've seen me. I *do* that. Because I am a selfish woman, David. I want there to be peace and kindness and people being polite to each other and not unhappy. That is exactly what I want. And sometimes, you know, if I fight very hard, if I use all my nerves and all my body and soul . . . sometimes an ugly thing doesn't happen. But sometimes, I fail.'

'Yes, we all fail sometimes.' He thought, Am I listening to some kind of principle here? He kept listening.

'Ugly and terrible things do happen. Hob died. You *know*. David, you have never let me make any bones about loving Hob, as I did. I truly did. You don't make any bones about loving June, either—with all your heart. And when you were young, too. In the good time.'

'I know, Abby,' said David humbly.

'So I fought not to believe in that horrible thing. But he did have it and he did die of it. And in pain. So when I couldn't make it be untrue, did I behave so badly?'

'No, darling. You did not.'

'Well, that is the *way,*' said Abby. 'And I've been fighting, all day. All this day. I've fought to understand him and forgive him, since this morning. I tried to think that Ladd and Felicia had eloped, you know. And that Rafe was all upset because he didn't approve. That didn't seem enough, so I even . . . Oh, David, it is funny, in an awful way. Maybe, I thought, that girl had gotten herself pregnant, or was saying that she was, and pressuring him. And that was the way to understand the things he said, and the way to forgive them. I even tried to eat that.'

'*Eat* it?'

'Yes. Yes. Like a dream,' she said impatiently. 'The way you eat a dream, in the morning. You have to take it *in*, into your fabric. It takes time.'

'Yes, I see.' David marvelled.

'But even so, even so . . . I couldn't get away from Ladd, this morning, saying some things to me. I would be very very glad to forgive them and forget them. But you see, when something breaks, why then it is broken. You can say that you forgive and forget but the break is still a break; it can't be mended.' Her

183

voice fell very low. 'That's how I know what Rafe is feeling now.'

David tightened his arm. 'You can't put Humpty-Dumpty together again? So Rafe says.'

'And he is right. I lost my child, my own little boy, that I can remember from the sight of his tiny tiny fingernails, all the way along. This morning, right in this room. Well, I suppose I only heard about it. I had already lost him. So that's gone now. And it never can come back.'

David was feeling he knew not what. Sadness and relief.

'That's why,' she said fiercely, 'I don't want fighting. That's why I fight fighting. Something always gets broken, and broken forever.'

He thought she would weep now, but she did not weep yet.

'It isn't,' she said, 'that I don't want to help him and understand him and love him, forever and ever, or that I wouldn't. But I cannot help him, I do not understand him, and if I am to love him . . . it has to be . . . not the same. And I don't know how it will be. So, David, will you? I need you to do it. Will you please do what is best to be done for this boy?'

'I'll do what is best, the best I can, Abby.'

So she lay upon his breast. 'Don't leave me,' she wept. 'I feel so lonely.'

'I won't leave you.' He was her rock.

'Well, he thought to himself, I seem to have the mandate. Gary's uncle tells me to

184

'straighten the boy around.' Aaron leaves me with it. The young cop 'guesses I'll take care of him.' Rafe leaves the boy, and Abby too, to me. And Abby needs me, to do what is best. I am the rock. My job.

Hob, old friend, he thought, Hob Cunningham, how would you do it?

It was late. They went upstairs. The house was quiet.

*   *   *

Ladd Cunningham had stripped off his clothing, his mind a greyness, shot with little disconnected flashes. He forgot about a shower. His normal cat-neatness was gone. Gone. Extraneous. Unimportant. He couldn't think what was important as he got into his bed. It must be night. Yes, he was going to bed. Therefore, it was night. He put out his light. As he turned on his right side his cheekbone hit the stone. He pushed it with the palm of his hand in one sweeping motion and the stone slipped over the edge of the mattress and was gone, without a thud, softly down among the trailing bedclothes. It seemed to him that he had lost something and he had better find it, but what he had lost was something he had never had so he would think about it tomorrow.

CHAPTER FOURTEEN

Very early the next morning, while David was at breakfast, the phone rang. It was Walter Douglas. 'The boy home, is he?'

'Yes, he came home.'

'And all right, is he?'

'I wouldn't say that, exactly. If you mean physically, he is all right.'

'Well, there was a little something. Just by a fluke, I caught it this morning.' (A ticket for speeding, thought David. But that was not it.) 'Call came into the man on the desk yesterday afternoon from some fellow—owns a sporting-goods store.'

'Sport—'

'Now, I don't say this is going to mean anything, necessarily. But the report was that some kid was in there trying to buy a handgun.'

'A gun?'

'That's right. Well, this fellow didn't like the smell of it. Said for one thing, the kid didn't know one type of handgun from another. He didn't sell, of course. Couldn't, legally. He thought he ought to notify somebody. Now, he didn't get the kid's name or licence number, unfortunately. But he says dark hair, dark eyes, medium tall, and driving a blue 1961 Corvette.'

'And what are you going to do about it?'

David said sweetly.

'Well, now, this kid may not have been your kid. No proof that he was. We could take him there and let the man see him. But he didn't get the gun, at least not that one. So there's nothing we can act on.'

'All right. Thank you,' said David wearily.

'But watch yourself,' said Gary's uncle.

David hung up. *Watch yourself?* (It was an expression that he despised.)

Get rid of! The echo came double. Gary had said that. Ladd had said that, in reverse. David couldn't believe it.

But he had to believe it. You don't believe on proof. You believe on probability, on pattern, on too many coincidences, on instinct, intuition, a certain clicking-down . . .

And nothing to act on?

Nothing? he thought. The boy has done *nothing?* What has he done? Let's see. Impolite at dinner. (Nothing.) Phoned the police with talk of murder. (No proof that he phoned and no confession.) Rude or worse to his mother. (Just how, she may never say.) Told a cruel and vindictive lie about the neighbours. (Not checked yet.) Tried to buy a gun. (No proof that it was he.) Wanted to 'get rid of' David Crown. (But he doesn't mean anything *too* bad.)

Yet I, and his mother (God help her), and the neighbours, and the police, and the psychiatrist, and even the cook in our kitchen, believe that this boy is sick, and now I believe that he is dangerous. Still, can no one of us or all of us together, act to keep him from doing great and worse harm *until he does it?* That is one hell of a note, thought David Crown.

In a moment, he reached for the telephone. As he dialled, David became bitterly amused. Modern man, rock and hero, what does he do in the face of danger and responsibility? He reaches for the telephone.

Nevertheless, David made some calls. But he did not call Rafe Lorimer. A phone bell ringing in that house would be too cruel if it bore no news of Felicia, safe and found. So he stirred himself and walked out of this house and over to speak to Rafe, old-fashionedly, in his person and his flesh.

*   *   *

He was coming back through the hedge, three-quarters of an hour later, when he saw Ladd Cunningham, in swim trunks, standing at the pool gate, rattling it rather angrily. 'Where is the key?' the boy demanded.

David came towards him, giving him full attention. Nice-looking boy, not too tall, rather slim but well muscled, not flabby, well tanned, healthy-looking. His nose a trifle long, like Hob's. His chin a trifle short, like Abby's. His dark eyes—like whatever ancestor's dark eyes. Inside—who could say?

188

'The key's not here,' Ladd said. Young lord of the manor, wishing his morning dip, somewhat annoyed. Nothing abnormal in that. That's if you did not count his mother, and one, two, three, maybe four other suffering people whose lives this boy had touched and altered for the worse.

'I'll get the key,' said David heavily. 'I have it.'

He went into the house and upstairs and found his own swim trunks. As he changed, he thought, I wish I had the key to unlock that boy.

He had been awake during the night and some of his night thoughts still held firm. To encourage Rafe to a lawsuit, just in the hope that during the slow grinding of the machinery of the law it would appear to some authority that this boy must be put where he would get psychiatric treatment. No. Not at the price of tormenting poor Rafe and the little girl (if God willing she was safe somewhere). The price was high, and gain not guaranteed. And what, he had thought in the night, would the boy be doing in the meantime?

Now, in the morning, there was an added feature. The boy, in the meantime, would be trying to murder David Crown. How did the victim find the key to unlock his murderer's intention?

David got into the trunks. He was fifty years old, but not too far gone to seed. Pale, yes.

189

Modern—he fought by desk and telephone. No athlete, he. Yet he was not without his skills. Not without his principles. Not without his faith.

These old texts, thought David, keep coming back to me because my father and my mother sent me to Sunday school, a long time ago. Yet . . . 'I will maintain my ways before Him.' And that I will, of necessity. Because the only key I have is the key that I am.

Abby had breakfasted and was on the terrace when David came down in trunks, towel and robe. 'Not the office?' she exclaimed. 'Oh, then I won't go to my luncheon.'

'I called Mike Palermo,' David said. 'Gave him a jolt by dropping the morning on him. But I think he'll cope. He may do.'

He had a momentary glimpse of a difference between himself and Hob Cunningham. David trained people up and then trusted them. Hob, to the last, was personally riding herd on his wild young men.

It was a sweet morning, in Hob's castle-keep. Abby, in a blue dress, sat in white chair. The roses were pink. Up the steps drifted the tanned boy.

'You went over to see Rafe, didn't you, David?' she said.

'Yes.'

'She isn't home yet, I suppose.'

'No. But Rafe is better this morning. Mrs. Wells is there. It seems, or so she says, that

Felicia has done some baby-sitting and therefore does have some money of her own.'

'Oh? Oh, I suppose that's good.'

'It's *better.* And Rafe isn't alone in the house, at least not now.'

*   *   *

Rafe was being stern and reticent, this morning. He would not hash things over. Yes, he had gone to Abby to explain the trouble between the children and to protect his daughter, who had the right to reject a boy's attentions. The boy had reacted insanely, in Rafe's opinion. Then and there. But Rafe would not soil his mouth with repetition. He understood, he said loftily, and he would do nothing, say nothing, simply wait and pray— until Felicia came home.

*   *   *

'Can't the police find her, David?' Abby was asking.

'They haven't. I called.' (The boy was near enough to hear.) 'I called the hospital, too. Mr. Harper had a good night but he can't have visitors today.'

'I'm glad,' said Abby gravely, 'that he had a good night.'

Now the boy was near enough to speak. 'How about the key?'

191

'Good morning,' said his mother.

'Hi.' The boy scarcely looked at her.

His mother said to her husband, 'David, be careful. You really shouldn't swim so soon after breakfast.'

'I'll be careful,' David promised. He started towards the pool and Ladd followed.

Ladd said, 'What's the idea? Why did you take the key?'

'So that Felicia Lorimer wouldn't drown herself in *this* pool at least.'

'What?'

David said nothing. He closed the gate behind them, leaving the key in the padlock.

'I don't get it,' said Ladd angrily.

'You mean you don't understand?'

'What did you *say?*'

'I'm pretty tired,' said David, staring soberly at the water, 'of trying to understand you.'

Ladd ran to the deep end and arched off the board. He surfaced and swam in a fast and beautiful crawl.

Showing off? thought David. Yes or no? I don't know. Or care.

He lowered himself to the coping and put his feet into the water, his old white feet. Ladd made a tumbling turn and raced back to the board end and helped himself out on his arms in one quick twist.

David thought, That was the truth. I'm tired of trying to understand. I am also tired of being devious, of influencing people, of leading them, as I led those women last night. I am tired of tact. Tired of trying to outguess reactions. Tired of pulling my punches. In my business, if I want to know something, I inquire.

So he asked, conversationally, 'Did you manage to get hold of a gun at all?'

'A what?'

'You heard,' said David wearily.

The boy sat, dripping.

'You want to get rid of me?' said David, in a moment. 'With a gun, for instance?'

The boy got up and out upon the board. He began to bounce on it, making it rattle. Then he landed hard on both feet and made the board still. A foxy look took over his whole face. 'What's wrong, sir?' he said innocently. 'Are you feeling guilty about something?'

'I'm pretty tired,' said David, 'of worrying about who is guilty of what. Aren't you?'

'Who worries about it?' the boy said. 'Some are. Some aren't.'

David lowered himself into the water grimly and struck out across the length of the pool with his old-fashioned, middle-aged stroke. When he was three-quarters of the way across, the boy's body sailed over his head in a high twisting dive. David made it to the other side and pulled himself around the rim of the pool by the use of his hands. He climbed out at the board end and sat, dripping. The boy came knifing back the length of the pool, swift and easy. His brown hand caught the coping, not a yard away.

'Swim competitively, do you?' David asked him.

The dark eyes were on his face. 'Why not?' the boy said contemptuously.

'Speed or endurance?' (No answer.) 'Let me guess,' said David. 'Speed?'

The boy pulled himself out of the water twisting away, landing with space between them. 'In spite of all that stuff you said the other night,' he said slyly, 'I wonder why you care.'

'Oh, I can't say that I care, passionately,' said David. 'Mild curiosity. How was Hob in the water? I can't remember.'

The boy became rigid.

'He was my friend,' said David, 'before you were born, and I'll speak of him when I like.'

'Not to me you won't,' the boy snapped.

These exchanges of open rudeness were something, at least. David said quickly, 'If you have got it in your mind that your father was murdered, get it out. He was not. If you have got it in your mind that I did it, get it out. I did not.' He expected nothing much from a statement of facts, but he would state them.

The boy said, 'Oh. Yes. That bothered you, didn't it?' Now the foxy look was back, and the eyes were bright.

David said, deliberately, 'But if it isn't in your mind, in the sense of reason, then there's nothing you or I can do to get it out. A trained man like Aaron Silver—'

'You might as well keep still about that damned doctor,' Ladd exploded. 'You're not going to con me into anything.'

'That's right,' said David. 'Neither you nor anybody else. I'm too tired. I'm not going to stand between you and anything, either.'

'Between me and what?'

'Between you and the consequences of what you do.'

The boy looked furious. 'What *I* do!'

David went right on. 'There is a principle involved. I guess you could call it the masculine principle. Cause and effect. Action and reaction. All right, if you told that nasty lie about the Lorimers, then no matter why you did it, there goes your reputation. And if they need money, it will be your money that they get, out of your inheritance. And if anything very bad happens to Felicia, you can expect some very bad trouble. I won't stand between you and these consequences. Your father might have. I don't know.'

The boy had that yellow look.

'Don't you have any idea of consequences?' David asked him. 'Don't you know what you've done to the Lorimers? Don't you care?'

'The Lorimers. The Lorimers. I'm tired of hearing about the Lorimers.'

David looked sideways at that face. He said, 'I'll admit that I believe, without the proof, that you did it. I'll get the proof, however, before I act.'

'You believe what you want.'

'That's what you are doing? You want to believe that I killed your father?'

'No, I don't want to.'

'Then why don't you find out? That's what I can't understand. Why don't you use your brain?'

'Just don't you worry about my brain.'

'I don't think there is anything the matter with your brain. But something may be wrong with your feelings. I'm not a doctor. I only want to get you to a doctor.'

'A person who doesn't feel that you're just adorable,' said Ladd jeeringly, 'must be crazy?'

'All right,' said David. 'Why don't you get on with it? Go ahead. Try to kill me. Then you'd get to a doctor for sure. The police have doctors. How about right here?' David was angry, and knew he was angry, and let himself be angry. I'm tired, he thought. I am damned tired of 'understanding' this kook. Let him understand me.

'I'm a little bigger and heavier,' he went on, 'and not as decrepit as you may think. You'd have trouble over-powering me on land. But I am a bum swimmer, as you can see. In the deep water, you'd have quite an advantage. Maybe you could drown me. It's all laid on, very nicely. Your mother has already warned me.'

196

'You're faking!' the boy shouted.

'How so?'

'You won't get me that way. *I* know what you want to do.'

'I've told you. I want to get you to a doctor.' David turned around and slipped back into the water. He began to swim his clumsy back stroke, watching the boy. He was a little frightened. He thought, The boy *could* do it, as a matter of fact.

But the boy did not do it. The boy stood up. For a moment David thought that he would jump in. But instead he sat down on the diving board. He sat very still, staring at the tree tops.

David lumbered around in the water for a minute or two, then he climbed out and sat, panting slightly. Now what? he thought. Have we made an advance here? Or did I descend to a childish level that has done harm. What's the consequence?

Somebody shouted, 'Hey, Ladd? What do you say?'

'Hey, Gare . . .'

Gary Fenwick was coming along the drive outside the fence.

Then Ladd said to David in a tense and demanding fashion, 'You were my father's brother, weren't you?'

'What?'

'You heard.'

'Yes, I beg your pardon, I heard.' David was baffled. 'Hob and I were room mates, best

197

friends.'

'Brothers?'

'If you mean fraternity brothers, yes, we were that, too.'

'Just don't kid me,' said the boy softly. 'Just don't kid me, Mr. David Crown.'

'That's a deal,' said David.

Gary burst through the gate. He let his slacks fall, even as he stripped his tee-shirt over his head and leaped (it seemed) instantaneously into the water with a mighty splash. The board clanged. Ladd's body flashed. There was a great hurly-burly in the pool.

David picked up his towel and his robe and went out of the gate without looking back.

The balance had swung. He was again a reasonable man. Going backwards over the course, he was wondering. What if Ladd had not tried to buy a gun? What if Ladd had not told the lie about the Lorimers? What if all Ladd knew about the phone call was what he had heard and seen when the policeman had been there? What if he had *correctly* divined that David had been 'bothered'? (As he had been, on Abby's account.) I must have looked, thought David, scared and even guilty.

Then, what if the one whose notions were askew was not the boy, but David Crown?

Would not a boy who disliked his stepfather (which, in all sanity, he was entitled to do) mightily resent the presence of a psychiatrist in

David's office that day, when it might very well have appeared to him that he had been lured into the meeting? And be further offended when Aaron came to dinner, *correctly* divining that Aaron was, in part, there as a spy?

Had anything the boy had said, just now, been in any way irrational of itself?

No. If you looked at the whole exchange from the other point of view, there had been only one thing that was even mysterious. What the boy had asked about the fraternity. Surely, unimportant.

As David came up on the terrace, where Abby was, he thought, But she knows. If she would tell me what he said to her, then I might have the clue. It had upset her. But . . . there again . . . how little it took to upset Abby.

'Could you talk to him at all?' She asked him anxiously.

He could not answer. He shook his head, in doubt.

'But look at them! They are like puppies.' The two boys were wrestling at the end of the pool, with grunts and cries, like any two boys anywhere. 'It doesn't seem possible,' said Abby. 'I wonder if Rafe Lorimer could have made some silly mistake.' Rafe Lorimer was, in fact, the man who could.

David said, 'I'll make sure. Mr. Harper may be available tomorrow.' He would not ask her what the boy had said to upset her. Shaky ground. This way, the way of checking up with the testimony of a witness, an identification of the boy who had told the lie, this was the better, surer, more rational way.

Abby had her hands clasped, holding off, he thought, with all her nerves, some ugly thing. 'Felicia is such an odd child,' Abby said. 'I never have understood her.'

How shall any of us, thought David, understand or be understood? What a ridiculous ambition! He told her that he was going to the office after all. Abby said she would go to her luncheon.

CHAPTER FIFTEEN

When David came into the house again, at a quarter past six o'clock Abby called to him from the library. David turned into that room and found her lying on the sofa, full of woe.

'Oh, David, I went to see Rafe.'

'Oh, Abby . . .' (He wished she had not.)

'He breaks my heart. He wasn't angry with me, or with anyone. He was s-saintly. Poor Rafe. He swears he won't set foot in his studio . . . He looks so old. I cried. I can't sit to the table, David. Cleona is bringing me a tray. I won't want much. Oh, where is that girl! Why doesn't she phone him, at least? How can she be so discourteous!'

David bent to touch her and give comfort,

200

when she saw something over his shoulder. She raised on an elbow. 'Ladd? Cleona will have your dinner on the table,' Abby said loudly to her son. Then, 'David, you'll stay with me?'

David straightened his back and turned to look. Ladd was dressed for dinner, informally, but immaculately. The dark eyes watched. Abby's hand had seized David's, and he could feel her pleading.

He said, 'I'm sorry you went over there. Let Cleona bring you your bite and you be quiet. Ladd and I will sit to the table.'

The flesh of her face seemed to fall.

He said, gently, 'Yes, that's best.' Her lids fell over her fear.

'So I'll just wash,' said David briskly. 'Ladd, tell Cleona fifteen minutes, will you, please?'

The boy blinked. 'Yes, sir.'

As David walked past him to go upstairs, he heard Abby say piteously, 'Ladd, will you please? I need to be quiet.'

'Of course, Mother,' he answered politely. Indifferently?

The boy turned. He stood, looking up the stairs.

*   *   *

Then the two of them were at the table. There were the normal 'thank you's' and 'please's' as they settled to the meal. David had collected himself. His normal antennae were out. He became aware that he had the boy's attention. Ladd was, somehow, examining David Crown with fierce interest.

Finally David said, 'I'm sorry about that set-to this morning.' A faint change on the boy's face alerted him. 'That is a courteous phrase,' David added, 'but let me put it a better way. *I* think I made a bit of a fool of myself. I don't know, yet, whether I am going to be sorry.'

The boy's mouth quirked. He ate a bite. He said, 'Mother thinks discourtesy is the only crime.'

David sensed the behind-the-scenes, confidential amusement that he disliked. It made him think of Dr. Jones. 'You might have mistaken her meaning just now,' he said thoughtfully. 'About Felicia Lorimer. Because your mother values courtesy so much, she believes there must be some very great and overpowering distress that makes Felicia leave her father in his present misery.'

The boy said, 'What misery is Cousin Rafe in?'

'The misery of knowing that she is very unhappy and not knowing whether she is safe.'

'How do you know,' said Ladd, 'that it was a lie?'

David stared. The boy had jumped eight steps. David said softly, 'It's unbelievable.'

'Why is it?'

'Do you believe it?'

Ladd shrugged. 'A lot of stuff goes on.'

And there it was. Something jumped reason, and any rules of evidence, to a conclusion. And David thought, He did it, all right. This damned brat, sitting to this fine table, in his clean clothes—and that poor heartsick girl, God knows where or how! Reason caught up and posed the question. How does he know what the lie was? Who would tell him?

'What did Rafe do to you on Monday morning?' he said sharply.

'Pardon?'

'And what did Felicia *ever* do to you?'

'Oh, not a thing,' the boy said, with a writhe of his mouth.

David wanted to slap it. But he reached for his wallet, took out a card and put it on the tablecloth. 'I forgot to leave this for you,' he said coldly. It was Aaron Silver's card.

The boy's glance flicked at it. He did not touch it. They continued their meal without conversation. The card was on the table.

Cleona came in to take their plates. 'You all want this, Mr. Ladd?'

'No, no,' he said, carelessly. So Cleona took the card away.

'You don't think you need the doctor?' David said, with excellent control. 'You chose to cause such pain, such damage, and now you choose to pretend you don't even know that the story you told is untrue. Still, you're not sick, you say?'

'I feel okay,' the boy said sulkily.

'Why then,' said David, 'the only thing for me to do is treat you as if you were perfectly well.'

'Why don't you? For a change.' The eyes were lit with something like relish.

Cleona brought their dessert. When she had gone, David said, 'All right. I'll tell you what I am planning to do. I am going to talk to Mr. Harper tomorrow, and I'll take your picture with me. So I will find out. When I have the proof that it was you who did this to the Lorimers, there will be the consequences I told you about, and one more that I haven't mentioned. Until you are cured of the viciousness that made you do a thing like that, you will not come into Cunningham Company. Not on November twenty-sixth or ever.'

The boy said, startled but sullen, 'That's what you think.'

'That is what I'll see to.'

'And who are you?' said Ladd angrily.

'A man—'

'Oh, you bet! Cunningham Company is *Hob* Cunningham's Company.'

'Hob Cunningham is dead,' said David, 'but Cunningham Company is a living organism. Too many people are involved to let you go in there and kill it, as you would, because you are not only ignorant but also either vicious or unstable. I promised your father—'

'I'll bet you did!'

'He asked me—'

'I'll bet he did! I'll bet he asked you to take over everything, everything! Including my mother.'

'Yes, he did,' said David flatly.

'You're crazy!' The boy was sobbing. 'How stupid do you think I am?' he shouted. 'You think I don't know . . . ?'

'I think you are just about as stupid as you can be,' said David, '*unless* you are sick. Will you answer some questions?'

'No.'

'Are you going to cry?'

'Don't be so damned . . .'

'Most people cry, when they need to cry,' said David. 'You've got tear ducts, like anybody else.'

'You've got such crust!' The boy gasped.

'Well? First question. Do you think I killed your father?'

'I know it,' the boy said stonily, dry-eyed.

'Then you are wrong. Ask the doctors.'

'They'd cover.' His face was taut and haughty.

'I see. A conspiracy, eh? So you won't come with me to the hospital where your father died and talk to the nurses and the doctors?'

'No, I won't.'

'That's stupid,' said David cheerfully. 'Answer this question? Did you, in a fit of rage or whatever fit it was, tell that dirty scandal about the Lorimers?'

'Let the Lorimers mind their own business,' the boy said in a furious voice. 'What does it matter? Listen, shall I tell you how I know?'

'I wish you would.'

But the wailing woman's voice turned both their heads. 'Oh, don't! Please don't!' Abby was standing in the archway to the hall, her hands clasped, her eyes filled with suffering, 'I could hear. And you mustn't! Oh please, don't fight! You tear me to pieces. When I love you both . . . Please . . . *don't* do this!'

David pushed at his chair to rise and go to her. Then all his senses bristled. He heard the boy say mechanically, in a dead voice, 'I'm very sorry, Mother.'

Cleona burst in from the kitchen way, bearing a pot of coffee. Her eyes were rolling. She quite obviously expected him to go to Abby. Abby expected it. The boy expected it. And David knew that this scene had been played many times before.

But David Crown was not Hob Cunningham.

He settled down. 'Cleona,' he said calmly, 'will you see if you can help Miss Abby, please? Just put the coffee down.'

'David?' Abby whimpered. She looked ready to fall.

'If you could help her upstairs? The doctor did leave some pills, I think? I'll be up—as soon as we have finished our dinner.'

'Yes, sir.' Cleona scuttled to catch Abby's swaying form. But Abby did not fall. 'You are *wrong*, David,' she said strongly.

'Just try to rest,' he said kindly. 'I'll be there.'

Abby turned her back. Cleona began rich murmurings, as they went away.

David turned to Ladd Cunningham and inclined his ear. 'Yes? You were saying?'

The boy stared at the table. He put both hands to his middle. 'Oh, no. *You* can say.' His eyes were not focused on anything.

'You were going to tell me . . . ?' David took up the coffee-pot and poured. His hand was steady.

'Nothing. Never. Stand on your feet. Oh, you bet. Speak up. Sure. And sit down and shut up. Think you're the only, only man and you say "Go ahead, go ahead," but you won't get out of the way . . .' The voice broke. 'But I didn't . . .'

David was out of his depth and he knew it. He poured cream. He took the sugar spoon, scooped sugar from the bowl.

'Well, I'll kill him, then,' Ladd said dully. 'That's okay. I know I have to.' He was holding his middle, as if it hurt him. But the dark eyes were focused, now, on the spoonful of sugar. 'It's easy enough,' Ladd said, 'if that's what you have to do.'

David's hand carried the sugar to his cup. The sugar fell into the coffee. The spoon

207

clattered back into the bowl. He said, 'Ladd . . .'

The dark eyes came up. No way to guess what they were seeing or waiting to see. David took the cup but his fingers were damp. The handle slipped, the cup fell, the hot coffee flooded the table.

He shoved backward quickly and rolled the cloth to make a rim and keep the damage where it was. He looked at the boy. The boy seemed dazed.

'Wow, you scared me!' said David honestly.

A most peculiar expression crept on the boy's face. David had no clue at all. The door-bell rang. Neither of them moved.

David said earnestly, 'I can't help you, Ladd. I don't know enough. Will you please go where someone can help you? You need not feel that you "have" to kill anyone. It isn't necessary.' (The bell grew impatient. Cleona was upstairs.)

The boy bent, holding his middle.

'Are you in pain?' said David.

'I don't have feelings,' the boy said. 'Or anything to say.'

David dared not touch him. He sighed and rose to stop the noise of the door-bell that kept ringing.

Gary Fenwick was at the door. 'Hi, Mr. Crown. Could I please speak to Ladd?'

'Well, I don't . . .'

'Hey, Ladd,' sang out Gary. 'Listen, Ron and Charlie are outside. Charlie's driving.

We're going on down to the Alley Cat, have a few beers, listen to the combo. So come on, buddy.' Big Gary, dumb and innocent, young and exuberant—normal.

David looked behind. Ladd Cunningham was in the hall, standing up straight enough. He still looked dazed.

'You finished dinner? Then come on.' Gary was full of energy.

At this moment Cleona called, from part-way down the stairs, 'Mr. Crown? The telephone for you.'

David had not heard it ring. 'Thank you. I'll take it in the library.' He started to walk.

Gary said, rather bewildered, 'It's okay if he goes, isn't it, Mr. Crown?'

God knows, thought David, I don't. He said, 'Let him speak for himself. Excuse me.' He went into the library, towards the telephone.

He heard Ladd say crossly, 'I'm coming. I'm coming. What's the big rush, buddy?'

'Well, listen, the guys are out there . . .'

David thought, Well, his peers. Maybe they can help him. And at least, Charlie is driving.

Aaron's voice said on the phone, 'David, what in hell do you think you are doing?'

'Aaron?' David heard the extension click. 'Abby called you, did she?'

'She did. She says you and the boy are shouting and fighting. What are you trying to do? Send him up the wall?'

'And if I could,' said David, 'you just might

209

come with the butterfly net?'

'Listen, old friend,' said Aaron chidingly, 'you are meddling with something you don't understand.'

'Agreed, that I don't understand. Denied, that I am meddling. I live here, old friend. Furthermore, everyone, including you and Abby, has dumped the job on me, to deal with the boy.'

'Dave, you cannot get into shouting arguments with these poor people. Surely you know better than that?'

'Surely I have the currently fashionable ring in my nose, you mean?'

'What's your point?' said Aaron shortly.

David sat down in the desk chair, there in the library, and leaned back. 'I would like to make a point,' he said, 'I would enjoy it very much. Are you listening?'

'That's my business.'

'All right. I would like to know what goes on here? What kind of civilisation are we getting into? Sure, I know the pitch—be gentle, kind, and understanding with these poor people. Do not for one moment allow them to feel that they are unworthy or unloved. Although they may be both. No matter.'

David was winding up and letting go. He was connected with a mind he knew and respected. Aaron Silver was his friend. 'Just roll with all the unpleasantness they cause, pity their hatred, forgive their cruelty, tolerate their total selfishness? Never mind what they do? Just don't call it wicked? Although it may be. No matter. Now, what is all this? A system of grinding the faces of the rich?'

'Come on, Dave—'

'No, you keep listening. I mean the rich in spirit. Those who don't pity themselves too much or too often, who survive the shocks to which all flesh is heir, who meet what they have to meet and are not made ill by life. They must stand still for whatever the weak, in their weakness, take a notion to do?'

'What's your solution?' said Aaron. 'The whip?'

'I don't have a solution. I'm not trying to cure this boy. That's for you to do. But I want a couple of answers from you, Doctor. First, do you expect every member of every family to be a trained psychiatrist?'

'No indeed,' said Aaron sweetly.

'Then answer this. The ones who cannot take this brawling world, the way it is, are the ones you'll cure, if you can catch them, by changing their attitudes, bolstering up their qualities and so on—until they *can* take this world? Isn't that your objective?'

'You could put it that way.'

'Ah, but us lay persons, in all our human ignorance and stress and struggle, *are* the brawling world. Wait, I'm developing something here. Some day this poor Ladd is going to have to learn to get along with so-called reality?'

'Yes.'

'Well, I,' said David, 'happen to be real. So I do not "meddle" when I simply refuse to be less than what I am.'

'*Less?*' said Aaron sharply. 'The lay public is going to have to learn some fundamentals, Dave.'

'What fundamentals?'

'As you say, understanding, not anger or fear.'

'And to me, it's pretty horrible to contemplate the day.' David was feeling giddy and gay with relief from pressure, now that the boy was not in the house, and he went racing on. 'Okay. Say I, and everyone else . . . we understand. Fear is gone from this world and so is anger. Here I'll be, busily understanding your poor sick psyche and taking great care not to damage your self-esteem. Meantime, you, of course, are doing the same for me. Now, will you tell me how we can possibly *meet?* When everybody pulls his punches, I'll tell you what is gone from this world. Honesty. And trust with it. And any chance of a friendship between two human beings. Damn it,' said David, 'to a friend you better be able to say what you really think or he is no friend. Just a manoeuvrable object. Furthermore, you got to watch out, because *he* is manoeuvring you. He has to, because everybody is mad— including me and thee. Although ME may be madder than thee, old friend, and a much more interesting case.'

Aaron began to laugh, rather helplessly. 'In the meanwhile,' he sobered, 'you had better take it easy.'

'You don't quite know, yet, what it is that I have to take easy. Abby?'

'She hung up, long ago.'

'I hope so, because Abby doesn't know this. The boy tried to buy a gun yesterday. He not only thinks I killed Hob; he intends to kill me.'

'Do you know why?' said Aaron in a moment, cautiously.

'Not I,' said David. 'And is there a "why" that a meddling layman can ever discover?'

'Don't be bitter,' said Aaron absently. 'How do you know what you just told me?'

'Oh, I can't prove it. He says he "has to".'

'*Says!*'

'Well, now,' said David, 'in among the shouting there was a little meat of communication. There's another fashionable idea. You can't possibly mean anything if you don't keep your voice down. What's become of the old human impulse to get up on your hind legs and yell? Why—'

'How did he come to say that?' Aaron brushed David's nervous nonsense aside.

'I don't know. Then, there is the Lorimer thing. You heard about it?'

'No.'

So David told him. 'Is that enough?' said

David seriously, at the end of his account. 'Once I've got the identification, can we then do whatever one does that will force him into a treatment?'

'You've got a . . . bad situation there.' (Aaron evaded?)

'I thought so myself,' said David dryly.

'The lie he chose . . .'

'Aaron?'

'Yes?'

'I don't know,' said David. A glimmer in his mind fled as he pursued it. 'I wouldn't be so certain.'

'We don't go in for certainties,' said Aaron, a little tartly. 'Your ideas of what we do go in for may be—as you put it—merely "fashionable".'

'Correct me where I'm wrong,' said David, cheerfully. 'What now?'

'How did he come to say he "had to" kill you? Is that what he said?'

David searched his memory. 'He said, "Well, I'll kill him, then".'

'Kill *him?*'

'Yes.'

'You were there?'

'Just the two of us, at the dinner table.'

'What had he been saying before that?'

'Hard to remember,' said David and realised he was echoing Cleona, 'when I couldn't follow. Let's see . . . Something about "You think you're the only, only man . . ."'

There was more.'

'Old friend,' said Aaron.

'Yes?'

'I don't know.'

'That makes two of us.'

'Will he be around the house tomorrow?' Aaron became brisk.

'As far as I know. Of course, I *don't* know.'

'I'm coming out and bringing a colleague. A young man. May be the right man among the lot of us. You and Abby both stand by. I'll try to get there around noon, at the latest. I'd make it first thing in the morning but I want to be sure to have Joe with me.'

'All right,' said David, 'I'll try to keep my mouth more or less shut until then. Thanks Aaron.'

'Well . . . try to keep more or less alive, will you, Dave?'

In spite of this remark, David hung up feeling very much better. Now he must go up to Abby.

But he could hear Cleona bewailing the disaster on the dining table. He went to explain whereupon Cleona's cries of dismay became croons of reassurance. David saw the sugar a brown ruin in the bowl. He put his finger into the mess and then to his lips. It tasted like coffee and sugar. Jumpy? he asked himself. He grinned at Cleona. For some reason, she grinned back.

215

CHAPTER SIXTEEN

Abby was sitting in her rose-coloured chair, with her head back, her face sad. 'Where is he?' she asked in a sad voice.

'He's gone off with Gary Fenwick and the gang. I should think that's all right. Aaron is coming tomorrow, at noon, or sooner, and bringing another man with him. They will know, I suppose, what to make of it all.'

'I am sorry,' she said woefully, distantly, 'but I had to.'

'I know that. I think you did the best thing.'

Her head came up. 'Do you?' Her brow puckered, her mouth trembled as if she would either laugh or weep.

'And I don't break easily.'

She smiled, with tears starting. 'I'm glad we are not going to fight.'

'Abby, to disagree is not so terrible.' He took her hand. She squeezed his; she was pleading. He said, 'But please, don't ask me to do *my* best in *your* way, darling. Especially when you have said that you can't do the job at all.'

'And *I* was thinking of scolding *you*,' she said in her strange mixture of humour, and childishness, and truth.

'Disagree with me,' he invited. 'I am only saying that I can act by my own judgment or I

216

can defer to yours, but I can't do both at once, when they differ.'

'Oh, mercy,' said Abby. She put her head back. He couldn't tell what she was thinking. 'Don't leave me,' she murmured.

He said nothing. He held her hand.

'Mercy,' she said, 'and kindness. He has to know that we love him.'

What if we don't? thought David. But he said, 'We'll see what the doctors can do, tomorrow.'

'Yes, tomorrow.' She smiled and sighed.

David kissed her lightly and left her. She was going to read a while. He went downstairs and into the library and found his own book. Something had been said that started up that glimmer in the recesses of his mind, but it fled again. He wondered if Abby thought that the boy would be healed miraculously, in a minute, tomorrow. He didn't know what Abby thought. Mercy she advised. Kindness she decreed. Love she assumed. But these were *very* precious and quite rare and not easily come by. Like honesty. Like courage.

And there was one thing Abby thought with which he disagreed. God bless her, she thinks that 'fighting' breaks people apart. Yes, sometimes. But sometimes, on the contrary. Sometimes, they are revealed to each other. Alas, what always breaks two people apart, or never lets them come together in the first place, is the lie. The condescending lie. Damn it, thought David, all by myself, I am related to that boy. But I've been pulling my punches too long. We ought to meet.

Well, never mind, be quiet, wait for tomorrow. He began to read. The door to the hall was open. His armchair faced the door. If the boy came home, he would say a kind 'Good night.'

He read until eleven o'clock. Nobody disturbed him. David went up to bed.

*   *   *

Ladd Cunningham came walking under the trees at midnight. It was pleasant to be a lonely shadow, slouching along the sleeping town. Only he was aware. All the rest were fools in dusty death . . .

He went around to the terrace door, turned off the downstairs light from the top of the stairs, and walked along the wing, from old habit. He opened the bedroom door and felt for the switch. The shock disoriented him for a moment. Where am I? Panic. Everything was gone. What to grab on to! Then he realised that he was in the guest room, his old room, by mistake. He left the light and stumbled to the other door, and put his own light on.

Now he was very tired. He fell upon his bed, just as he was. The thing in his pocket was hurting his hip. He lay, inspecting pain.

He was quiet at first, sitting with the guys at the table. But the joint was jumping and, in all the noise, his silence wasn't noticed. He was floating, that was the trouble. Trying to grab on, somewhere. Not to anything in this place. But to anything. He had a feeling that something very funny was going on in the world. He kept squeezing in and ballooning out, in a kind of rhythm. He'd squeeze in, feeling desperate, with an inner screaming after what it was that he absolutely had to do. Then he'd balloon out, with a funny feeling of satisfaction. But that didn't dare last long. He might balloon way, way out—too far. So squeeze. He was beginning to feel sick at his stomach when Ron and Charlie went off to the Gents and Gary said in his ear, 'Hey, Ladd, my Uncle Walt was over today. Listen.' (Yes, in the smoke, under the music, listen.) 'He's checked everything out. Honestly, everything. And your Dad died from a heart attack, actually. Listen, he says you can believe it. So okay?' Gary beamed and began to work his leg to the beat the way musicians did.

And Ladd grabbed on. Oh ho, just as he had expected! Cover! He grabbed on to something hard.

All right! Okay! Nobody else would do it, so he would have to do it.

He felt better. He kidded around, after that,

the secret hard inside. He did a lot of figuring and thinking, without anyone knowing it.

Going home, he made Charlie let him off in the bad part of town. That was amusing. They didn't know his secret. They thought they knew what he was after. They had to respect his purpose and his nerve, not only because it went against the rules for good children, but because it really was risky down here. Those houses were filthy. So they shrugged it off. They let him go. They acted bored. They couldn't say that they were scared.

But he wasn't after what they thought. (And never had been.) He got what he was after.

He lay upon the pain for a long time. Then he rolled over and took the object out of his pocket. He put it on the shelf behind his bed, next to the stone. He touched the stone.

Suddenly he got up, tore off his clothing, went to the bathroom, put on his pyjama-bottoms, switched the light off.

He got into bed. His hand groped for the cold stone. Stone cold dead. Left it, and touched the warm knife. The switch-blade. He had known he could find some kid who had one, down in that part of town, and so he had. A skinny kid, with white eyes in the street light, who took his money.

Warm, from his own pocket. Destined for warm flesh. He took it from the shelf and slid it under his pillow and then he was floating again.

Certainly funny when David said he was scared. You didn't say that. Sure, you'd get scared . . . and tear ducts like everybody else. Squeeze. Not too far, the balloon. Couldn't bear it. That's what his mother always said.

He wondered if she was alive.

*　　　*　　　*

The telephone screamed alarm in the night.

David sat up and put on the light and grabbed the phone before it had rung four times. But Abby, in her own bed, was already up on her elbow, terrified. One did not know, did not know, what might make a telephone scream in the night.

'Hallo,' croaked David.

A voice was already speaking, insistently. 'Is this Mr. Crown?'

'Yes?'

'Mr. Crown, this is Justin Lorimer.'

'Oh. Oh, Justin.' David repeated the name for Abby's benefit and saw her sink back and hold her hands to her pounding heart.

'I'm sorry if I woke you but I have to know what's going on.'

'Yes, that's all right.'

'Dad just called me. He says the police are looking for my sister.'

'Yes . . . they—'

'Why?' said Justin.

Oh, that bright force! There would be no

221

fooling this one, David thought. He began to cough.

'Mr. Crown?'

'Yes, Justin.' David coughed. 'Minute. I'm half asleep. What did your father . . . ?'

'He is in a state,' said Justin rather impatiently. 'I guess he got himself worked up, he had to talk. He told me why she went. But he said you'd been a big help. So I want to know from you, why the police?'

David put the instrument aside to cough again.

In Ladd's room, Ladd lay in the dark listening. He had picked up his extension on the third ring.

'I'm coming home,' said Justin.

'The police will find her,' David said, strangling back his coughing fit. 'Better than any of us can. Or she'll come home by herself. But to answer your question . . .'

'Yes, sir.'

'The thought was . . . although I'd say the danger was past by now . . . that she might have been in such a . . . state . . . as to harm herself. It just seemed wise to try.'

'That's what I was afraid of,' Justin said calmly. 'Did Ladd Cunningham tell that story?'

'The . . . old man is in the hospital. I hope to see him and make sure, one way or the other, tomorrow. But about that story . . . I have already talked to people . . .'

222

'Dad told me. Thanks. That part doesn't worry me. Who cares if some idiot wants to tell a lousy lie and make a damn' fool of himself? But see, if it was Ladd . . . Well, Felicia thought he was the greatest.'

'She did?'

'I told her to stay away from him.' Justin began to speak with some heat. 'Oh no, she thought she was the only one who could understand him. She was all set to go hunting around, Saturday night, so she could find him and hold his little hand and listen to all his little troubles. I told her she was stupid. Oh no, somebody had to talk to him and let him talk.' Justin became cool again. 'What worries me, if he did a thing like that to her, it could have hit her pretty hard. She was making such a big hero out of him.'

'I see. I see,' said David in misery. (Rafe had got it backwards, then? One ought to have suspected.) 'But they haven't found her. She should be all right.'

'Maybe.' Justin took the reassurance sceptically.

'She left a note,' said David, in a stronger voice. 'I saw it. She did say a couple of days.'

'Right.'

'Tomorrow is only Wednesday. Well, thanks a lot, sir. Probably she's got more sense. He sure isn't worth it. I'll see you.'

'Justin, need you . . . ?'

'My father is in a flap,' said Justin. 'He isn't

223

the most competent person in the world. And you've got troubles of your own.'

Justin hung up.

David, holding the phone, a bit bemused, heard distinctly the click of an extension cutting off. It was Ladd in Ladd's room, or a burglar in the library. But there was no burglar in the library.

'Justin's terribly upset?' Abby begged this not to be so.

'He says he is coming home.'

'Oh, that long, long drive,' Abby said. 'Oh, dear!' She sat up. 'Oh, David, look! The light! Look . . . in the guest room.' They could see across to the other wing. 'Why is that? Is Ladd in?'

'He is in,' said David. 'I'll go turn off the light. I'll see.'

'Oh, please do,' said Abby, trembling.

David didn't bother with a robe. He went out into the upstairs hall and around the elbow of the house, guided by lighting streaming from the bedroom door behind him. The guest room door was open, shedding light. Nobody was in there.

David clicked the switch. Now he stood in half dark. The other door was closed and no light rimmed it along the cracks. No sound within.

But the boy was in there, and awake, and he had listened. David hesitated. A very strong impulse took hold of him. He must open that door. He must speak. But he hesitated. Don't meddle, he said to himself, remembering his expert's advice. So he did not . . .

But yet . . . David made his way back . . . but yet . . . If that was my boy, or one of my girls, in such deep trouble behind that door, could anything keep me out?

The boy's mother said, 'Is he all right, David?'

'Everything is quiet,' he told her.

Back in his bed, he turned his thoughts to Justin's long drive, and he knew what he had better do to Ladd's car in the morning. He had better immobilise it. Suggest this to Abby?

David rolled. Damn it, am I his father now, or am I not? You can't be two different things at once. It'll drive you nuts.

CHAPTER SEVENTEEN

David got to the hospital at 9.30 on Wednesday morning, but he was not allowed to see old Mr. Harper. It was out of visiting hours. Furthermore, the patient was not reacting as well as had been hoped, so he could have no visitor but his wife and she only between two and four. So sorry.

David had no argument. So he drove to the little white cottage and found old Mrs. Harper. The timid little lady was in a state of anxiety, over which she had pasted a stubborn hope. Yes, she would try to remember, and if the chance came, yes, she would show the photograph to Mr. Harper. Mr. Harper was going to be all right. It was just a matter of time. He would have to be careful, perhaps, but she and Mr. Harper would not mind that.

David could see, in her, Abby's way. Hold on, with muscle and nerve. Insist. Insist that what you want is so. Then the old man's feet would be again on the single path of peace, the well-pruned narrow way to their survival in this brawling world that grew younger and younger all around them. He went away, sad for her, and quite sure that she would forget.

Ten o'clock. Could he spend an hour in the office? No, better not.

He thought, It is like having a bomb in the house, the mechanism of which you do not understand, so that you had better not tinker with it, yet you cannot go away and leave it and you cannot throw it out. A hell of a note!

It was a quarter past the hour when he turned into the drive and braked his car in a hurry. The Cadillac had been backed out of the garage so that it stood like a dam across the way. Dingy from disuse, it looked derelict and strangely squatty. David walked to it. All four tyres were flat. Three of them seemed to have been slashed with a knife. Hob Cunnigham's car was immovably in the way. David went in at the kitchen door. 'Cleona, what happened?'

'Mr. Ladd, he fit to be tied when his auto*mo*bile won't go. He bound he'll take his daddy's. But it won't go, either. Seems like them tyres all busted.' She gave her report calmly, but there was fear in her eye.

'Where is he now?'

'He up in his room. He won't let me in to make the bed.'

'Where is Miss Abby?'

'Oh, she out on the terrace, now.'

'I didn't see her.'

'She there. She sitting in the corner. I'm real glad you come home, Mr. Crown. Miss Abby, she say to bring some good eatings over to poor Mr. Rafe Lorimer. But I didn't want to go and leave her.' There was the faintest question in the last sentence.

'Good for you,' he said.

Her hands went to a round tray on which a napkin covered something in the shape of a mound. Her hands were nervous.

'I'm here now.' He nodded comfort.

He hurried through the house and out upon the terrace. Abby was, indeed, sitting in a corner, an especially shady spot beyond the chimney. She wore a white dress and sat in a white chair knitting on a sequined sweater.

'Good morning again. I only just came down. Isn't it *warm*?' said Abby, all together.

'Are you all right?'

'Of course.' She bent to her work and David

looked down at the top of her head, Oh, Abby, darling, liar! Sitting in the deep shade on a cool fresh morning, where you cannot see the Cadillac. But you could not miss it from our bedroom. Just holding, insisting. Nothing frightening, nothing ugly, must happen or have happened.

He said, 'I'm going up to talk to Ladd.'

'Oh, should you?' The puckered brow. The troubled eyes. 'David, you look so big and stern. Please, you mustn't scold him.'

'For what, Abby?' he asked quietly.

Her lids fluttered. She abandoned the lie. 'After all, you did something to *his* car. Surely you can under-stand.'

'That doesn't make it right for him to damage your property.'

'But darling,' she cried, 'I don't *care*. I *love* him.'

'Ah, but then you should care.'

'No, David. I beg of you. You mustn't upset him. Not now. Aaron is coming.'

'I don't intend to upset anyone.'

'You are upsetting me,' she wailed. 'I'm trying so hard to be calm . . . and to eat . . . eat the idea that my son is sick in this terrible way. I'm so confused and worried. I need you.'

(A rock, am I? thought David. Or a piece of putty in those pretty helpless hands? Oh, Hob old friend, what were you?)

While he pondered, she dropped her hands and the work on her lap and said, 'David, I

228

know you've tried very hard and been so patient. But you don't love my son. How could you? You are not responsible for his behaviour, either. How could you be? Just please . . . go on being . . . ?'

'Patient? Kind?'

'Yes. Please.'

But David thought, What am *I*?

'I was going to do better than that, Abby,' he said, 'according to my lights. It seems to me that I committed myself not to kid him. So I think I owe him an apology for what I did to his car, without his knowledge and without explanation. I am also going to tell him that those doctors are coming.'

'Oh, David, no! Please . . . he won't like it! Why should you?'

'Because . . .' (David was going to say, Because we are setting a nice little trap for him here, conniving at it behind his back. Oh for his own good, oh yes, and in mercy and kindness and love—of a sort. But it smells like a kind of betrayal. And it is condescending. And I won't do it. I will maintain my own ways. He couldn't say all that.) He said, rather sadly, 'Because I am responsible for my behaviour, Abby.'

'But, David, after all, you are *not*—'

'Not his father?'

'That's true.'

'I have married his mother. I live in the same house. I am his elder. I am also a male. I

229

think all that obliges me, enough.'

She said, 'He might . . .'

'It's between us,' David said gently. 'We've met, Abby.'

She looked off at the roses and her throat worked. He went into the house.

* * *

Ladd was on the stairs, looking down morosely.

David looked up and said, 'Good morning, Ladd. I should have told you. I didn't want you driving off to parts unknown this morning. Dr. Silver and another doctor are coming to talk to us all.'

The boy looked down, dull of eye.

'I had to go out, you see,' said David. 'That is, I thought I had. But Mr. Harper can't be seen yet.'

'Harper?'

'The old man.'

'The one in the car?'

'That you talked to.'

'Yes, about the Lorimers.'

'Why did you?'

'I . . . don't remember why.' The boy was slack, spiritless. He was dishevelled. His clothes looked slept in. 'I didn't know where you were,' he mumbled.

David took note of his condition and it seemed to him to be symptomatic. He said,

'You go up and down, don't you?'

'Well, it's . . .' The boy took his hand off the banister and put his palms parallel. He moved them near, then apart. 'It's more—in and out,' he said and then, pitifully: 'You know?'

'I get a kind of dim idea,' said David.

'Ah no,' said the boy, mournfully. 'Ah, no.' He hung his head.

'Why did you cripple the Cadillac?' said David.

'Because it's rotten.' (A spark in the eyes?)

'Well, it has to be moved. I'd say, call a dealer.'

'Dealer?'

'Sell it.'

The boy had one hand back on the banister. He took one step down. 'You want to get rid of it?'

'It isn't mine.'

'His.'

'Your mother's. But she'd sell, if you said so.'

'Would she?'

'You could talk her into it. What do you think it's worth?'

'I don't know.' The boy came down another step.

'Rather keep it?'

'It's . . . my father's.'

'It's a piece of machinery,' said David, 'and it's been neglected. Come on down, and we'll take a look under the hood.'

231

The boy said suddenly, 'It sounded like a damn' truck.'

David grinned.

But the boy's head jerked. A high wailing was suddenly on the air. It was outside of the house. It was primitive. It raised the hair. David ran to the terrace.

Cleona was staggering up the steps into the garden, her arms crossed on her bosom, wailing to the sky.

David took great strides. He caught her by the shoulders. 'What's the matter?'

'Oh, Mr. David . . . Oh . . . Oh . . . Poor Mr. Rafe Lorimer . . .'

'What is it?'

'The police came. All the neighbours is out. They done took him.'

'Took him?'

'Oh, that poor child. Oh Miss Felicia, what did she want to do that for? She done jumped off a roof and she dead. Poor, poor child.' Cleona began to cry tears.

David looked up. Abby was as white as her dress and the chair.

Ladd Cunningham, in the terrace door, was yellow. 'And the neighbours say somebody done told some kind of mean old story and break her heart. Oh, poor child! Just a little child and she dead so soon!'

Ladd flashed around, turning his back. He stood and seemed to quiver. Then he broke and ran into the house.

David said to Cleona sharply, 'You're doing a great job of breaking the news.' Her sobs choked.

David left her and went to Abby, who was rigid. He picked her up out of the chair in his arms. 'Cleona,' he called, 'get Dr. Jones on the phone and tell him to come here right away.'

'Yes, sir. Yes, sir.'

Abby's skin was genuinely thin. David was afraid for her. He carried Abby indoors and Cleona scuttled past them. 'Where did they take Rafe?' David demanded.

'To the morgue.'

'Why?'

'To see if it was.'

'To *see* if it was! Aren't they sure?'

'I don't know. Oh, her poor daddy, he got to go see if it's his own child.' Cleona was going to wail again. 'Get on that phone,' snapped David.

Abby moved in his arms.

'Hush,' he said to her. '*Now* is the time for you to disbelieve. Suspend your belief. Hold on.' He carried her upstairs and to her own bed. He didn't know what was going to happen. He wanted her safe, and out of the way.

'It might not be?' Abby whispered, as he put her down.

'I'll call. See if they know yet.'

Cleona was on the downstairs phone. David heard the door-bell.

'Even if they do, don't let *me* know yet,' Abby said, with cold-blooded self-wisdom. 'Let me fight it my own way. It prepares me.' She closed her eyes. Her breathing was all right. He left her.

No sign of the boy. In his room, David supposed, and God knows how he is. He raced down the stairs and opened the front door. It was Gary Fenwick.

'Go up to Ladd's room,' said David quickly. 'We've just heard.'

The big lad looked shaken. 'I just heard, too.'

'Is it true?'

'It's some young girl. They took Mr. Lorimer for him to identify—'

'All right. Go up to Ladd, Gary. I want you to do that.'

'Well, sure,' said Gary. 'But some of them are saying . . . It wasn't Ladd, was it? They say somebody was telling a dirty rumour. He wasn't the one?'

So much, thought David, for my influence. The story is around. He said to Gary, 'Yes, I'm afraid he was the one. And I don't think he had better be alone.'

But Gary's face bloomed red and he stepped backwards. 'Then I don't want to have anything to do with him.'

David, with no time to persuade, closed the door in that shocked and righteous face.

Cleona came out of the library. 'Doctor is

coming.'

'Get to your room and get hold of yourself,' David ordered. 'It may not be Felicia Lorimer at all.' Cleona ducked her head and passed him. David started for the library, to call the police, find out. He heard the boy's voice.

'David?'

'Yes?'

The boy was at the top of the stairs. He had something in his hand. He said, 'I have to, now.' He started down. The thing in his hand was a knife.

'Do you really?' said David calmly. It was so pitiful that he had to keep himself from laughing.

'Now?' the boy said pathctically. 'Now, I do. Otherwise, everything was for nothing.'

'It may not be Felicia Lorimer. That's not certain.'

'Yes, it is,' the boy said mournfully. 'I know.'

'But let me check.'

The boy, coming slowly downward, said, 'Did my father get to die his honourable death?'

David was rooted where he stood, his heart contracting. 'Yes, he did, Ladd.'

'Do you swear it?'

'I swear it.'

'Then there isn't any honourable way, for me. There is the only way.' The boy had stopped. He shook. 'It has to be me, then.'

'No-no,' said David, not sharply, but

235

judiciously. He was wondering how he would get up those six or seven steps and seize the knife. The blade was out. Could the boy hurt himself? Yes, he might. David kept his gaze steady. As long as he held the boy's gaze, the boy might not try. But the boy's eyes knew this. They seemed to beg his pardon before they looked away.

Then, like a tiger, a bright and burning force leaped into the house.

CHAPTER EIGHTEEN

It swept from the terrace door to the bottom of the stairs. Its very passage blew David into a backward stagger.

Justin Lorimer put one hand on the banister, one foot on the lowest stair, and lithe and strong and beautiful as a tiger, he paused and gathered to spring. 'There you are,' he said with relish.

The boy on the seventh stair had the knife in his right hand. His left arm crossed his body to hold to the banister. His face lost its pathos. It hardened. He said, 'You don't need to bother.'

'No guts?' said Justin. 'Put your toy away. Or don't. I don't give a damn.'

David said, with newly caught breath, 'Have you checked, Justin? Have you checked?'

236

'No,' said Justin, not turning, continuing to be taut. 'If I was sure, then I'd kill him. Right here and right now. Shall I come up?' he said to Ladd. 'Or are you coming down?'

Ladd's face was changing again. It was as if he saw, far away, some kind of light. He did something with his hand and the blade of the knife disappeared into its handle. He swung his arm backward and the knife thudded down upon the tenth stair. Then, he seemed to be gathering to spring.

'He's not himself . . .' David began.

'I don't give a damn who he is,' said Justin, not one muscle in his fine body relaxing. 'Let him think he is Napoleon. For what he did to my father and my sister, I'm going to beat the living stuff out of him.'

Ladd Cunningham said, as if to explain, quite patiently, 'He has to.'

David saw something white flutter to the top of the stairs.

'Abby? Stay back.'

Neither young animal seemed to hear, or relax one muscle, and the force went between them, very strong, very clear and pure. David stepped back and put his body against the front door. He thought, Yes, they have to. Justin must. Ladd needs the pain. They know, these boys. Abby doesn't understand these things.

But Abby was coming down the stairs. She was on the ninth stair already, white dress against the wall. She was wailing, 'It can't be Felicia. It cannot be.'

Justin's shoulder rippled. Ladd shifted a foot. They were both totally concentrated. David couldn't visualise a fight on the stairs. They would tumble down. Surely they would tumble, locked and threshing. Himself concentrated, he tensed. He awaited the explosion and the tumble and Abby, to be left where she stood.

Justin took three steps up, quick as a cat, and tensed again, poised, concentrated. Ladd's neck seemed to lengthen.

But Abby cried out, 'Ah, don't! Justin, dear! Ladd, my darling!' She put her foot on the eighth stair and shuffled sideways, then the other foot on the seventh stair. She turned and put the power of her beloved self between, and her son screamed with a kind of ripened desperation that burst out of him, *'Get out of the way!'* He flashed around like a dancer, turning away from her, but completely around, and as his body made the circle, quickly and violently, his body struck hers and Abby tumbled.

She had no footing at all. She went like a stone, thrown. She slammed into Justin and he went backward with a yell.

Justin fell on his back, his head on the floor, his legs on the stairs and one of them bent most unnaturally.

Abby fell on her back, overlying him at an

angle, her head downward, thrown back on the neck, just missing the wall. Her two feet were together by the banister. Her arms were strangely at her sides, her skirt decorous. She looked like a lady doll.

David got there. 'Don't move, Abby. Not for a minute. Hold still, Justin. Are you hurt, Abby?'

'My back,' she said clearly.

'Where, darling? Where?'

'In the middle. A little lower. It feels broken.'

'Oh God! Justin, lie still, can you, boy?' David could see, where Justin's left leg lay so crookedly, that it could not lie so unless that bone were broken. 'I'll get help. Abby, don't move.' He said to Justin, 'I'm afraid for her life. Can you bear it?'

'I guess I got to,' Justin said between his teeth.

'David looked up behind him. Ladd Cunningham had retreated upward and was sitting on the tenth stair, holding to the balusters like a very small child illegally out of bed, watching his parents give a party.

David bellowed, 'Cleona!' He did not dare leave the spot. He had to leave the spot. She did not come soon enough. What could Cleona do if she came? He felt frantic. He had everything to do.

Very well. *Do it.* He clamped down. His mind responded to discipline. The cord, the

239

long cord! He moved carefully around the fallen. Had to risk something. The best gamble was now. Quickly.

'Don't leave me.' Abby did not whimper. This was almost mechanical.

'He's got to,' Justin said. 'Lie still, Cousin Abby.'

'Am I heavy?'

'It's okay. It's okay.'

'Something always breaks.' Abby's voice was changing, becoming a little gay. 'Who said that? I think I said that. That was pretty smart of me.'

David was back. He had dared race into the library and drag the phone on its long cord as far as it would go, which was far enough so that he could put his head around the door-jamb and keep watch upon the bomb that still ticked, for all he knew, up there on the tenth stair.

He dialled emergency. His mind went double. What to ask for. How the boy might plunge, or stumble recklessly down, and complete the wreckage. Kill her.

Cleona peered from the kitchen door. She was going to shriek. She must not.

'Go away, Cleona,' he said to her sternly. 'Just keep quiet and go back. There's nothing you can do.'

His mind was adding up pros and cons. Quicker to speak directly. 'The hospital,' he said into the phone. 'Emergency.'

Abby said, 'He didn't mean—'

'Be quiet,' said David. If he could keep sound away . . . The clicking on the phone was loud in his ear. But the boy could not hear that. The boy could not hear . . . David jumped at the sound of the door-bell. He called out, 'Come in, whoever you are.'

Knob turned. Door cracked. Aaron Silver's head came through.

'Get in here,' said David, 'and don't do anything. Watch. Wait.'

Aaron and a younger man, who looked as if he had been playing football only yesterday, tall and broad, both of them came in. Neither said a word.

David began to bark his needs into the telephone. Ambulances. For two people. One a woman, with a possibly broken back. Send special equipment to move her. And a doctor. Urgent. Very urgent.

He put the phone on the floor. 'You've had medical training,' he said to Aaron. 'Tell me. Can she be moved now?'

Aaron went closer. The other man moved beside him. Neither asked how this had happened. Neither showed any shock. They moved, they looked to see.

'Pain, Abby?' Aaron was on his knee.

'It hurts terribly. I said that something always breaks. I didn't know it would be me.' Her childishness. Her own kind of courage. Her face was upside down to David. She

241

couldn't see him.

Aaron touched her ankle. 'Do you feel that?'

'Yes.' By her voice, one knew she knew the possibilities.

Aaron got up. 'I'd say we need more trained hands. The risk is there.' Aaron glanced upward at Ladd, who had his cheek pressed against the balusters childishly. Aaron did not speak to him at all.

He looked down at Justin, who was braced on his elbows with the sweat running on his brow. 'Can you hold out?' Aaron asked him with compassion.

'Yes, sir,' said Justin. 'I've got it made.'

Aaron's smile was tender. The younger man went nearer, and saying nothing, he sank slowly to his knees on the floor. Slowly, and very carefully, he thrust his big left arm into the triangle of space between Justin's shoulders and the first riser. He brought the arm slowly upward until it was giving some support.

'Better?'

'Yeah. Thanks. My leg, though . . .'

'It does seem to be broken,' said the young doctor casually.

Aaron said, 'They won't be long. What are they sending, Dave?'

'Ambulance. Maybe two. A doctor. Yes, and Dr. Jones, damn him, was called long ago.' Was it so long? David wondered.

242

He couldn't see Abby now. The big young doctor bent too near her. Heavy, heavy, over them all, hung the unpredictable. No one spoke to the boy.

'Take about six, eh, Joe?' Aaron was saying.

'It should,' said Joe. He spoke to Justin, 'If you want to pass out, I can hold you.'

'I never do . . . pass out . . . too easy.'

'Well, I'll tell you, you're entitled.' The voice was grave but easy.

It struck David that no one was speaking to Abby. 'Abby?' he said, not easily.

'She couldn't bear it,' said her son calmly. 'She's dead now.'

'Fainted,' said Aaron, quick and low. He did not move but David knew that he tensed. He knew about the bomb. David's mouth was dry. Let the boy be quiet. Let the boy cling to the balusters, frozen in shock. Let him not start to feel. Or speak. Or move. Or begin to realise. Or think of his sins. Or his wrongs. Or himself.

Three of us, he thought. Can't we pin him down, take him away, do something? No, not three. The big young man had, in compassion, got himself bound where he was, supporting Justin. And Aaron . . . the boy distrusted Aaron. How can I get up there? David pondered. Could I hold him if I did? Is there a word that can hold him? He could think of no word that was not too risky. Be quiet. Be still. Keep sound away.

'Where is my son?' Rafe Lorimer's voice

243

said loudly. 'They say he flew home. He came over here?'

And there was Rafe, coming in at the terrace door, like the family pet, without asking permission. In his paint-stiff trousers and an old white shirt, looking red-eyed, as if he had been weeping. 'What I have been through!' he cried with rich emotion. 'And it wasn't my Felicia. Some poor poor girl but not *my* girl. I am ashamed that I am glad. But I am glad. Where is my boy?'

David thought, We can't have this. We can't have questions. We can't give answers. We must not have rich emotions. Not now. It's too dangerous. Be quiet. Be still.

So he walked quickly. He said in a low voice, 'Rafe, go out on the terrace and sit down. Right now. Justin's had an accident but he is all right and help is coming. You cannot do a thing here. Do as I say.'

'But where is he?' Rafe was in the middle of the hall and the sight of two bodies, upside down, at the foot of the stairs, was not in his range. His voice began to swell. 'Where is my boy?'

David had his arm and was tugging at it. 'Be happy about Felicia. Go out there and thank God.' David was savage, in a low voice. 'And for God's sake, be quiet. I'll call you when it's time.'

Rafe was inert, resentful, about to protest. But a voiceless something made him look

244

above. Ladd Cunningham's face peered down, through bars. Rafe shuddered violently. His feet began to shuffle. As if he were the family cat, David put him out.

Silence. Cleona was silent and frightened, still standing in the kitchen door. David banished her with a gesture. She drew in one shuddering sob as she retreated. It was very loud in the silence. David was frightened. But he had better not be frightened. It was too dangerous. Aaron put a foot on the bottom stair. The boy stirred. Not Aaron. *My job*, thought David.

He said, 'And I'll get out of the way, too.'

He walked up the outside of the banister, his feet on the tiny ledges. He swung his leg over to the sixth stair. He sat down on the eighth. He wound his hand to a baluster and held on tightly. The boy's legs were under that arm. David took care not to touch them. He sat still. The bomb was to his back. But he was between Abby and the bomb.

The young doctor said to Justin, 'Where'd you fly from?'

'San Fran.' Justin had not passed out.

'Jet?'

'Right. Listen, I don't know,' said Justin, sweating, 'about this, too much longer.'

The young doctor took his folded handkerchief from his pocket and put it between Justin's teeth. He said, 'Those jets will sure scare the hell out of you, taking off.'

David marvelled. And his mind, going double, remembered the knife. It was behind him. All right. No matter. Sit still. Not much longer.

Now. A siren sounded and the door-bell pinged, simultaneously. Aaron opened the door for Dr. Jones. The one siren snarled and died as another was screaming upward on the scale. The noise was terrible. David held hard to the wood. He could sense, through his back, ripples of arousing.

Something impelled him to say, companionably and almost with enthusiasm, 'Watch this, Ladd. Watch how they work.' And his back was broad and strong enough, not to wince or startle.

Men came in, without any babbling. They were slow and meticulously gentle, but so decisive that they seemed to be working fast. Inch by inch, a folded blanket was slipped between Abby and Justin. Six men, holding the blanket's edges, synchronising their movements to a steady and exactly even effort, very very slowly and very very surely lifted Abby's arched body still in its very arch, away. Slowly and evenly, they carried her out of the house. Two men bent to Justin, who was letting himself moan a little. They did things to that crooked leg. They put him on a stretcher. They took him away.

It was Aaron who went back to the terrace and summoned Rafe Lorimer to go with his son.

As Rafe's wild crop of hair went by, underneath, Rafe was saying with rich emotion, 'What is happening to me and my children? Is there a curse on the house of Lorimer?' Aaron put him out, at the front door.

All the while, David sat on the eighth stair with a weight against his back. The sagging weight of the boy's body where he lay, warm and heavy, upon David's muscle and bone, breathing like a child when it's asleep.

Sirens wailed, going away.

Aaron said in normal voice, 'By the way, this is Joe McDonald. David, you'll want to leave now?'

'Yes, I must.' David stirred. The boy moved. David slid sideways, as the weight lifted from him, and turned to look. The boy's lips moved soundlessly.

Joe McDonald said, 'Ladd Cunningham is your name. How about you coming with me? I've got a little old Austin Healey outside.'

The dark eyes looked his way but the boy said nothing. It was David who said, 'Where would you take him? I don't want to leave him here alone.'

'Alone,' the boy echoed.

'Well, I had in mind a hospital, kind of,' Joe said. 'Where he can relax, and we can figure things out a little bit.'

'Are you a doctor?' the boy said. Life

seemed to go on in him, like a light bulb.

'That's what I am.'

The boy looked down, to his left side.

David saw the knife on the tenth stair. He leaned back, with one elbow on the tenth stair, not touching the knife.

The boy's long lashes lifted. The dark eyes were sombre. 'Is it because I am sick?' He was asking David.

'It would be good to know,' said David.

Joe said, 'This is an okay place. You wouldn't be alone. We can make some tests, and all that.'

The boy looked into the young face below. He turned again and the dark eyes searched David's face. 'Shall I go with him, Dad?'

David groped for phrases and discarded all of them. 'Yes,' he said.

CHAPTER NINETEEN

By five o'clock, they had put a set of tyres on the Cadillac and managed to turn it. Then, tilted on two wheels, all its lines spoiled, the big car went away behind the tow truck, looking like a monstrous baby carriage.

David turned, and saw Aaron Silver pulling to the kerb. He stepped quickly. 'How is the boy?'

'Safe,' said Aaron, smiling. 'Shall we put it

that way? Abby?'

'She's safe.' David did not smile. 'Will you come in?'

They went into Hob Cunningham's house. 'As you see,' said David, 'I am in sole possession. Drink?'

'Fine. It occurs to me that it might be useful if I knew what happened here this morning.'

David took him into the living-room and, when they had sat themselves down with drinks, David told it as briefly as he could.

'You seem depressed,' said Aaron.

'Oh, I am. I am. Consider the damages. Broken bones, lives, hearts . . . not to mention that the little girl is still missing. All on account of one miserable mixed-up boy.'

'Is Abby depressed?'

David drank deep. 'Abby is in the damnedest cast I ever saw. She'll mend, they say, and there'll be no paralysis. She doesn't blame him. She startled him, and he didn't mean it. It was essentially an accident.'

(Abby, who fought all ugly happenings but, when she had lost, behaved very well. Darling Abby, whom he loved. To whom he would, therefore, give all that he was. But no less.)

'You think he meant it?' Aaron was asking.

'I may give up thinking.'

'Nobody is guilty, Dave.'

'If I weren't too depressed to wiggle my mind,' said David, 'I'd give you a knockdown drag-out argument on that.'

Aaron smiled but said nothing.

In a moment, David said, 'All right. In a nutshell. If nobody is guilty, then nobody is any good, either.'

'I should have said, Everybody is guilty?'

'Not all of the people, all of the time,' said David. A chance. A choice. A risk, even. That's all I'm asking. He shook himself. 'What is the prognosis on the boy?'

'We are not witch-doctors. Tests to make, much to do, before we can even begin to sense the dimensions of his trouble. How can I say? He's at a bad age. Yet, we may have caught him early enough.'

David fiddled with his glass. 'Justin Lorimer is done out of a semester.'

'Too bad.'

'I'm partial to him. I think I'll offer Cunningham Company to Justin. He is a relative, of sorts. And I could train him up.'

'Yes, he might shape up,' said Aaron neutrally. 'He is a little like Hob, wouldn't you say?'

'May be,' said David. 'May be. Hob had a blind spot.'

'Justin has his.'

'I agree.'

'Still, who hasn't?'

David brooded. 'What would it do to a boy, Aaron, if he is told that it's a fine thing to live his own life and that he may and ought to, but if he chooses to do or say what his mother would rather he did not, she will suffer, unbearably?'

'*Some* boys,' said Aaron, who had listened intently, 'might get mixed up.'

'This boy!' burst David. 'Do you know what I think? He must have believed, when he was small, that she literally could not bear it. That she would die.'

'Possible.'

'What a spot to be in.' David sighed. 'There was sex in it, too, I suppose.'

'We'll help him look for what is there,' said Aaron placidly.

'Did he love his mother and hate his father?' asked David, with curiosity.

'Probably.'

'Then why does he want to revenge his father's death?'

'Because he loved his father and hates his mother. Probably,' said Aaron, with a twinkle. 'And, probably, he himself is both. Or doesn't know which.'

'If that's not witch-doctor talk! You pulling my leg?'

'*We* don't know,' said Aaron. 'The boy has to peel the layers and the contradictions from himself, by himself.'

'I'd like a plain fact or two,' said David grimly, 'if I'm not asking too much. For instance, why did he think I'd killed Hob?'

'He had to put a floating fury somewhere, maybe.'

'But he was going to tell me why.'

'Yet he didn't?'

'No, no, Abby came . . . ' David sighed, once more. 'Abby acts on a principle, you know. Sometimes she wins.'

'Don't we all, sometimes?'

'Not if we can't fail,' said David severely. 'I'll ask you a question, Doctor. And there had better be a plain answer. How does the layman deal with a bomb in his house?'

Aaron understood at once. 'I've seen bombs to which yours was a firecracker,' he chided. 'You didn't do too badly, old friend.'

'Old friend,' said David, 'I go by results. Which are extremely poor. You fellows better come up with some fairly simple rule or rules for the layman to *apply*. None of these layers and contradictions.'

'Alas,' said Aaron, 'we deal with the individual.'

'No universal rule?'

'Love?' said Aaron, tilting his head as if he listened to the word.

'On demand, eh? Just turn the tap and there she flows.'

'Didn't she?'

'What?'

'In your case?'

'Not me. I could have flayed him.'

'Why didn't you?'

'I didn't coddle him,' said David shortly. 'And I'll tell you somebody else I'd like to

252

paddle and that's young Miss Lorimer. For her discourtesy.'

'You want a fact?' said Aaron. 'All right. I told you on the phone, at about six p.m. on Monday, to try to get the boy into therapy. At twelve-fifteen p.m. on Wednesday, he went with Joe. Now, what do you want? That's fast work, old friend.'

'I didn't do it single-handed,' David said morosely. 'There were contributions.'

'Justin and the whip, you mean?'

'Love, too. Abby tried that.'

'Yes. His love for her. *That* love she tried.'

David looked at his old friend sourly.

'Gloom's the ticket, I see,' said Aaron, leaning back. 'But somebody loved him.'

David opened his mouth, but there came a tapping on the window. 'What . . . ?' He got up and opened the long glass. Felicia Lorimer stepped in and said breathlessly, 'Justin was *hurt?* Where is he? Where's my father?'

David stood still, but Aaron, jumped. 'Come in. Come in. Are you all right, Miss Felicia?'

'Of course. What's happened?'

'Why, your brother will be fine,' Aaron began.

But David looked down at the girl and, with a lift of his hand, he shut Aaron up. 'This is what happened, Felicia,' he said quietly. 'You ran away. Your father was frantic. He called your brother. Your brother flew home. When he got there, the police had taken your father

253

to the morgue. Justin came here to beat up Ladd. Abby tried to stop it. She was pushed downstairs and it broke her back and Justin's leg. They are both in the hospital. Ladd's in another hospital, for tests and therapy. I don't know where your father is. He *was* with Justin. The girl in the morgue, obviously, was somebody else. I suppose, for half an hour at least, your father thought she might be you.'

Felicia clung to the back of a chair and listened to him, motionless, all the way through. Only her face seemed to become tighter and whiter.

Aaron said, 'Sit down, Felicia, please. Don't blame yourself for all of that.'

But she did not move. She kept her eyes on David. He said, 'Why couldn't the police find you on Tuesday? Were you hiding?'

Her back straightened. 'Yes, I rented a room and said I was Felicia Cunningham.' She put up her chin. 'No, Dr. Silver,' she said clearly, 'I don't blame myself for all of that. But I'm sorry for it. Is . . . poor Abby going to be all right?'

'Oh, yes.'

Aaron started to say more but David said shrewdly, 'Your father ought to have known you had some money.'

'He did know.' (David nodded.) 'I said a couple of days. It is a couple of days. Why did the police take my father to the morgue?'

'Because you were missing and very

254

unhappy and talking "silly." Cleona told us.'

'I had to get over that,' she said. 'That's why I went. And my father wanted me away, you know. He didn't know how to arrange it.'

'Sit down,' said David, smiling at her.

Felicia sat down. (Aaron sat down and was still.)

'I thought it was best,' she said, 'to get myself straightened out first.'

'It's a good idea,' David said gravely.

'So I had to think. I had to pray. I sat in some empty churches. I believe in God.' She said this last sadly, as if no one would take it seriously.

'Why, so do I,' said David, as if this were not uncommon, but it was always pleasant to meet a fellow enthusiast. He sat down. 'Was it the lying story, in itself?' He was respectful, but not pulling any punches. 'Or because Ladd told it?'

She shook her head. Her face had lost flesh. She wasn't pretty. But there was something . . . 'Not because it was Ladd. It was the . . . idea. I mean, what you call the lying story. A lie can make you good and mad,' she said. 'Oh, the truth can, too. But of course, sooner or later, you'll have to take the truth. But it's—' She stopped and looked at Dr. Silver and back to David. 'That's only because you've been alone. Go on.'

She regarded him silently a moment. Then she said bravely, 'After a while, I figured it out.

255

It's something that could be just a little bit true—that shocks you.'

David nodded. 'Shakes you up,' he said.

Felicia held his eyes, in wonder. Then she said earnestly, 'I love my dad, but I manage him. I hate to, but I have to. Otherwise, he blunders around in my life. He doesn't mean harm.'

David nodded. 'I can imagine.'

She sighed. Her eyes fell. 'Well, I think I can manage, that's all.'

'The story isn't the problem now. Ladd is— discredited. It'll be on his head.'

'I know,' she said. 'And it's just for this winter, really. I'll be out of high school. I can get a job. And—he gets to working.' She looked down at her hands.

'Your father knows what the problem really is,' said David in a moment. (Aaron stirred, but said nothing.) David went on, 'He said to me that you can't put Humpty-Dumpty together again.'

'Did he?' said Felicia, looking as if she'd been enlightened. 'I'm sorry for him, then.' She began to bite her lips. 'I shouldn't manage him. I'll try . . .'

'Would you like to go to school in Europe?' David said. 'I'm sorry—for you.'

Felicia shook her head slightly, not to say No, but to say, Wait, discuss that later. 'Not for me,' she said. 'I'll be all right.' Then, with a look of sudden mischief, she said, 'Humpty-

Dumpty was an egg. Suppose it had already hatched?'

'Then she could fly,' said David quickly.

And Felicia smiled and her eyes danced.

The door-bell broke the spell. It rang again. Cleona must be out of hearing. David rose, reluctantly, to answer it.

'Mr. Crown, I'm sorry I kinda ran out this morning,' said Gary Fenwick, looking very unhappy.

'I'm sorry, too,' said David.

'Ladd's in a mental hospital, isn't he?'

'Yes.'

'Well, there was one thing, though . . .'

'What was that?'

'If anything happened to him, I was supposed to tell. So I . . .'

'Come in.'

'Hi, Gary,' said Dr. Silver.

'Hey, *Felicia!*' cried the big boy, with honest delight.

'Hallo, Gary,' she said courteously. She was twice as old as he.

'What was it you had to tell?' asked David.

'The trouble is,' said Gary, squirming, 'what I'm supposed to know, I don't guess I do know. But, see . . . he was pretty sure . . . well, he was sure that you'd killed his dad.'

'Yes, I know that he was. Do you know why?'

David could tell by the tail of his eye that this was news to Felicia, but she took it, said

257

nothing, made no gasp.

'Well,' said Gary, 'you know that box? That black box?'

'Yes?' David's ears pricked.

'Well, there was something in it, in a book, that made him so sure. A message from his father, he said it was.'

'What message?'

'He wouldn't show me. He said he was the only one who could read it.' Gary shifted his big feet some more. 'I know where the book is,' he offered, 'up in his room.

'Then will you get it?'

'Sure thing.' Gary made off. They heard his heavy feet on the stairs.

Felicia had laced her fingers and bent her head. 'Rafe!' said David suddenly. 'And Justin, too. I'll call.' He went swiftly into the library, by way of the door from this room, to call the hospital. He didn't know where Rafe was, but Justin must be told in any case, and Justin might know. Abby must know. And Ladd Cunningham. He needed to know that Felicia was safe.

Felicia lifted her head and looked after David Crown. Dr. Silver sat still, watching her face.

As David came back, so did Gary, bounding into the room like a retrieving puppy, bearing a leather-bound desk-diary. 'It was in here some place.'

'Thank you, Gary.' David took it. He did

258

not open it. 'They are very glad, Felicia. Your father is coming. You are to stay here.'

'I'll be glad to stay here,' she said gravely. 'Thank you.'

'Will Ladd get better, Dr. Silver?' Gary asked.

'We hope so, Gary.'

'He was my best friend,' said Gary solemnly. Nobody spoke. 'Well, I guess I better get going.'

No one detained him.

When he had gone, David opened the book. Hob's notes, appointments, reminders. He flipped the pages. 'These are pretty cryptic. Do you suppose Ladd thought it was a code?'

David had gone past the end of the daily notes into the blank pages—past where life had stopped, he thought—and there, at the end, was a section for names and addresses, cut to alphabet tabs. There, on the first of these, he saw Hob's handwriting, but unnaturally large, written in emotion.

'Here it is,' said David sadly. His throat was tightening. He gave the book to Aaron.

Aaron read it to himself. He began to mutter, frowning. Then he read it aloud, evenly, unpunctuated.

'A is for Abby B for the boy C for the company D for my Old Brother Death is his name AVE.' Aaron looked up. 'What is that? DAVE? Your name?'

'Oh, no, no, no,' said David. 'Hail!'

'Hail?'

'As in Hail and Farewell. *Ave. Ave.*'

'Latin!'

'Yes, yes. But the boy asked me if we had been brothers.' David sat down with his hand shielding his eyes.

'What he needed it to mean,' murmured Aaron. He looked at his friend, concerned. 'David?'

'Excuse me. I can't help thinking of Hob. He must have done that on his last day in the office. When he knew where he was going. Thinking of him that day . . .' David's eyes were hidden. 'He . . . as Gary would say . . . was my best friend.'

'I loved him so,' cried Felicia. 'I adored him. Everything he said or did. I was even jealous of Cousin Abby.'

They looked at her. 'Hob?' said David softly.

Tears slid on her cheeks. 'Why do you think,' she said to David, 'that I used his name? Once, on a terrible day, he said something true to me, Hob Cunningham did. And it was the best, most loving thing! Old Brother Death, he said to me. When my mother was dead and my father kept saying she'd gone to heaven. Yes, I know. But Hob Cunningham said it was *hard.* And it's very hard. *Life* is! So I loved him. I was so young. I see, now, I loved him—some impossible ways. *He* didn't know it . . . In my dreams, do you

260

see? Do you see?'

David nodded. He could not have spoken.

And Cleona shrieked in the hall. Felicia got up and wobbled to her. Cleona enfolded the girl and wailed for joy. And Felicia wept a little.

The men were silent. Then Aaron said musingly, 'And the boy didn't recognise his father's phrase?'

'In the years of the boy,' said David, 'there was Abby.'

'Who couldn't have borne it.' Aaron rose. 'Old friend, I must get home to my dinner. Rafe Lorimer all right, is he?'

'I spoke to him at Justin's bedside. He wept and he wailed,' said David softly, 'and he called upon the Lord to witness . . . that Rafe knew it, all the time.'

(Felicia was asking for a glass of milk. Cleona was delighted. They went away.)

So David said, 'Hob fathers a boy like Ladd. Rafe fathers a boy like Justin. And a girl like this one. What do we conclude?'

'What you already know,' said Aaron, with the faintest accent on the pronoun. 'That every child is a new and holy mystery and it was God who made him.'

'But we must raise them.'

'They grow. We train them . . . *up*, as you say . . . for a little while. But they are in the world, not in our pockets.'

'Ah, and that's risky?'

'Surely.'

'They meet what they meet?'

'They do. Some of them are lucky.'

'And choose?' David swept on. 'And the risk goes both ways?'

'For worse? For better? Surely.'

'Ah,' said David.

They walked to the front door together. Cleona's rejoicing and the girl's soft voice were a song in the kitchen. 'I see you paddled her,' said Aaron mildly.

'What?'

'Good night.'

'Thanks, Aaron, and good night. Oh, I meant to ask . . . When may I come to see the boy?'

'I'll let you know,' said Aaron fondly.

We hope you have enjoyed this Large Print book. Other Chivers Press or Thorndike Press Large Print books are available at your library or directly from the publishers.

For more information about current and forthcoming titles, please call or write, without obligation, to:

Chivers Large Print
published by BBC Audiobooks Ltd
St James House, The Square
Lower Bristol Road
Bath BA2 3BH
UK
email: bbcaudiobooks@bbc.co.uk
www.bbcaudiobooks.co.uk

OR

Thorndike Press
295 Kennedy Memorial Drive
Waterville
Maine 04901
USA
www.gale.com/thorndike
www.gale.com/wheeler

All our Large Print titles are designed for easy reading, and all our books are made to last.